PRAISE FOR THE WORK OF MARIO BELLATIN

"As an ever larger legion of readers—perhaps it should be said: of followers—has confirmed, Mario Bellatin, the artist of the air, is perhaps the strangest and most fascinating writer in contemporary Mexican literature—although here it must be said, likewise: of contemporary literature tout court*—unlike the majority of his generation, he insists on creating—on plotting—an unclassifiable, unpublished, slippery work, in perpetual mutation. Because Mario Bellatin is not a writer. Or isn't one in the restricted, impoverished sense of the term today.... Bellatin is a multiple, multifaceted, itinerant creator, overcome by a limitless curiosity and willing not just to experiment with his texts and acts but with himself, in order to escape the limits imposed by literary genre, by society and its conventions."*

—Jorge Volpi, author of *Season of Ash*

"Everyone talks about inventing their own language, but Mario Bellatin actually does it."

—Francisco Goldman, author of *Say Her Name*

"Mario Bellatin, who has the fortune or misfortune of being considered Mexican by the Mexicans and Peruvian by the Peruvians, [is one of the] writers without whom there's no understanding of this entelechy that we call new Latin American literature."

—Roberto Bolaño, author of *2666*

PRAISE FOR THE WORK OF MARIO BELLATIN

"The Large Glass *examines the purpose and form of biography through short works that seem drenched in an aura of pure memory. These are not set-pieces that, through hindsight's perspective on the big picture, artificially recreate the past. Rather* The Large Glass *is a journey through the twisting corridors of remembrance, where detail is distorted, features exaggerated, and meaning warped. The result is an utterly mesmerizing exploration of why and how we remember our own stories."*
—Christopher Phipps, Diesel Bookstore, Oakland, CA

"Once again, Bellatin manages to create a small book that's somewhat cryptic and confounding, but also perfectly satisfying—in a way that makes me wonder whether I actually read The Large Glass *or somehow dreamed it."*
—Kate Garber, 192 Books, New York, NY

"Here's a writer who very well may be the rightful heir to the Borges throne. His writing, the overall thrust of his work, seems determined to take a metaphorical blowtorch to the structures of narrative storytelling."
—David Gonzalez, Skylight Books, Los Angeles, CA

THE LARGE GLASS

by Mario Bellatin

Translated from the Spanish
by David Shook

PHONEME
MEDIA

Los Angeles

Phoneme Media
1551 Colorado Blvd., Suite 201
Los Angeles, California 90041

First edition, 2015

ISBN: 978-1-939419-49-1

This book is distributed by Publishers Group West

Designed by Scott Arany
Cover Art by Zsu Szkurka
Author photo © Eric Curtis, 2015, www.ericcurtisphoto.com
Grilled Cuy photo © Nestor Lacie, 2011, flic.kr/p/aD5w43, used under
🅭 Attribution 2.0, www.creativecommons.org/licenses/by/2.0/

Phoneme Media is a nonprofit publishing and film production house, a
fiscally sponsored project of PEN Center USA, dedicated to disseminating
and promoting literature in translation through books and film.

www.phonememedia.org
Curious books for curious people.

Other Mario Bellatin titles available
from Phoneme Media:

Shiki Nagaoka: A Nose for Fiction
Jacob the Mutant
The Transparent Bird's Gaze (ebook)

Forthcoming Mario Bellatin titles
from Phoneme Media:

The Uruguayan Book of the Dead
Taxidermied

A selection of films featuring and made in
collaboration with Mario Bellatin around the
world are available at www.phonememedia.org.

THREE AUTOBIOGRAPHIES

My Skin, Luminous

...on the outskirts of the tomb of Sufi Saint Nizamudin.

1 — During the time that I lived with my mother
it never occurred to me that adjusting my
genitals in her presence could have any serious
repercussions.

2 — I was wrong.

3 — Later I learned that she even asked other women
for objects of value so that they could see
them fully.

4 — Adjusted, choked, to the point of bursting.

5 — My mother taking advantage of my pain.

6 — Collecting objects without rest.

7 — Many times things to eat or small garments for personal adornment: plastic earrings or some thin cord clasped around her wrist.

8 — One time she acquired a pencil with which she colored her lips.

9 — The enthusiasm that lining her mouth caused her was so great that for a few moments she forgot my presence.

10 — I managed then to untie the strange garment that she had devised for our visits to the public baths.

11 — I was entirely exposed.

12 — A diffuse light illumined my flesh.

13 — I decided to jump in the water.

14 — In the deepest part.

15 — I broke through some obese women that impeded my path with their bodies.

16 — I was even about to cross into the section reserved for men.

17 — If I had managed it, I am sure that I would never have been received in the same way by my mother.

---

18 — I found myself on all fours.

19 — The water mixed with clay.

20 — If I had been standing it would have barely reached my ankles.

21 — I would remain exposed then again to the stares that make possible my current presence in these baths.

22 — The women rummaged through their belongings and managed, by means of the particular barter that my body propitiates, to contemplate me for the time they deemed necessary.

23 — Unexpectedly it occurred to me to turn around.

24 — My mother was still beside the washbasins of thermal waters.

25 — She remained absorbed in the ritual of outlining her mouth.

26 — The rest observed her carefully.

27 — Except for the obese women, who seemed desperate to leave the zone reserved for them.

---

28 — I dare to say that this scene, of my mother coloring her lips, was a spectacle foreign to the customs of the region.

29 — It seemed so distant from our custom that I could not control myself and I yelled at her.

30 — My voice was increasing.

31 — The splash of water against the cement canals emphatically distorted the words I was directing at her.

32 — I couldn't allow my mother's mouth to be more important than the spectacle that my testicles are capable of offering.

33 — But in that moment it appeared to be; even the obese women looked willing to break the rules and prepared to enter the thermal waters zone.

34 — That had never happened before.

35 — After a certain age and according to different body qualities, each had their assigned section.

36 — Only children and adolescents were allowed to go between them without permission.

---

37 — The first few times I grew accustomed to remaining under water many hours.

38 — During that time I hadn't yet experienced how excesses usually become prejudicial.

39 — I was still unaware of how very ancient surfaces become when they are traversed by liquid substances again and again.

40 — Discovering the marks that time produces over the textures is perhaps one of the most valuable teachings of these public baths.

41 — The only thing that seemed to escape that fortune of constant deterioration is perhaps my testicles, always willing for exhibition.

42 — My mother typically waited for me each day at the exit door.

43 — She looked content each time we came back together.

44 — She almost always kept the objects she acquired during the workday with her.

45 — She liked most of the gifts that they offered her in exchange, but she seemed to have begun to feel a special predilection for lipsticks.

46 — On more than one opportunity she woke me up in the middle of the night to show me her mouth colored purple or fluorescent fuchsia.

47 — It was difficult to be sure if that exalted figure was part of a dream or an action that existed in reality.

---

48 — My mother doesn't typically stop showing me her lips until I wake all the way up.

49 — On mornings like that it is difficult to return to a deep sleep.

50 — I remain between wakefulness and sleep.

51 — So I place in practice an old game—which has entertained me since childhood—that consists of removing my genitals, without the use of my hands, from the strange undergarments that my mother made me.

52 — This garment, which I must wear at all times without its presence being often noted, isn't exactly her invention.

53 — To design it she has followed a set of ancient patterns.

54 — I also know that her occupation of displaying her children's genitals is not her own invention either.

55 — It is an ancient practice for which not all women with children are qualified.

56 — In reality almost none find themselves in the position to go through with an exercise of this nature.

57 — From there, the tiny quantity of mothers of this type that exist today.

---

58 — In the district where we lived they had never known of the existence of such a woman.

59 — It had to be my own mother who informed them that, fifty year earlier, her grandmother's sister had become, as a product of this occupation, the most powerful woman in the zone where she grew up.

60 — There was some memory of her adventures.

61 — But no one, not even my mother, knew of that woman's final destiny, nor, least of all, that of the son that had gained her such prestige.

62 — "The rumors are true," my mother told me one morning when she had woken me up to show me her lips covered in an oily patina.

63 — "Many details about genital-displaying women are remembered, but everything about their exhibited sons is forgotten."

64 — Later I found out that they killed them mercilessly.

---

65 — I fell deeply asleep.

66 — I had many dreams, which continued over the next nights.

67 — I imagined the appearance of the women that grew rich offering those types of spectacles.

68 — Also that of their own sons.

69 — It was said that the genitals wound up being victims of the evil brought on by the jealousy of others.

70 — That from one moment to the next they began to dry up, until the inflated sack that held them was nothing more than thin and hanging innards, which finally detached itself from the body before the victim even became aware of what was happening.

---

71 — When boys lose their testicles in that way their mothers immediately flee.

72 — They carry as best they can the valuable objects they've gathered and typically head toward the mountainous zone.

73 — In olden times the law indicated the form of death for these boys.

74 — One of the most common ways was to leave the wound formed by the fallen scrotum untended.

75 — I found out about that method a relatively short time ago.

76 — The director of the Special School I attend described it to me.

---

77 — "Why am I enrolled in a Special School?" is a question that I never stop asking myself.

78 — I don't think that anyone has a sure answer, not even my companions in reclusion.

79 — They are content, like me, with knowing that I sleep in one of the central pavilions.

---

80 — My mother perhaps knows why she was so adamant to the director that she got me admitted.

81 — She seemed not to have enough with my repeated exhibition at the public baths.

82 — Growing rich with the objects she kept acquiring.

83 — Coloring her lips until she couldn't any more.

84 — Nothing seemed to be enough.

85 — Anyone who had seen her at that time would have thought that she hated me with all her heart.

86 — They would consider this the only option especially if they had appreciated the joy that was reflected on her face when the director finally gave her verdict.

---

87 — When the desire for me to join the Special School was born in my mother, we already visited the baths with frequency.

88 — In that epoch, a school of that type was perhaps the only solution that she could find to be considered a somewhat normal mother within our community.

89 — Perhaps thereby she found a way to overcome the neglect of my father.

---

90 — My father's lover had died soon beforehand, from a grave illness.

91 — She worked as a secretary at the public institution where he worked.

92 — I never knew if it was his secretary or with another employee.

93 — What I do know is that my mother suffered from the illness as if she had been developing it in her own body.

---

94 — I remember that some time after we were left alone—my father left us one winter morning—my mother began to undertake a series of experiments with my body.

95 — I imagine that she did so to more effectively ensure my entry to the Special School.

96 — At that time we had returned to live in the back room behind my grandfather's oven.

97 — Among other actions she placed some glasses on me through which reality became a jumbled, unrecognizable presence, capable of producing nothing more than a disagreeable dizziness.

98 — On other occasions she didn't let me breathe, covering my face with a pillow until I felt myself die.

99 — Once she tried to put my cranium into a skull she kept for unknown purposes.

100 — On a certain morning, when she discovered that I had bought candies with some money that fell in the street from a boy's pocket, she singed my hands in a fire she lit for the sole purpose of teaching her lesson.

101 — My mother finally got me accepted to the Special School after the first incursion we made at the public baths.

102 — Someone had told her that that visit was the only way to get the director to finally give her consent.

---

103 — At that time my mother was a truly poor woman.

104 — She didn't even have the purse that she now enthusiastically shows off.

105 — Just the two of us lived in the room behind the oven where my grandfather had always cooked the pigs for the community.

106 — Our bodies began to expel a smell that was nearly repulsive.

107 — My mother had begun to save toward the end of paying for the entrance fee to the baths, since at that time to afford such an expense was an almost unreachable undertaking.

108 — As we knew the visit was forthcoming, we decided to suddenly abandon the forms of cleaning that we usually practiced.

109 — We had to economize wherever we could.

110 — No water bought from the traveling hawkers.

111 — No bags with the leftovers of soaps, which some merchants in the community resold on the main street after using them, but not entirely, in the public baths.

---

112 — When we finally gathered the value of the entries we woke up before dawn broke.

113 — We quickly left the back room.

114 — We knew that the lines of people waiting to enter began very early.

115 — Many were merchants that went to visit those baths before beginning their shifts at work; there were also women of the highest lineage, who seemed to want to take advantage of the opaque light of dawn so that no one could clearly appreciate their bodies before being introduced to the water.

---

116 — On that first occasion we stayed inside for many hours.

117 — The gifts began to appear as soon as my mother took off my pants.

118 — From then onward we got free admission.

119 — We went as often as possible.

120 — So my body never again smelled disagreeably.

121 — My skin changed after a few weeks.

122 — Without anyone warning me it became covered with a type of patina, slightly viscous, and with a luminosity that for some is even more amazing than my own genitals.

123 — I never asked my mother what she thought about that peculiarity.

124 — I think that to have done so would have been an invitation for her to discover new possibilities for my body.

125 — I don't even want to think of the power that a luminous skin might have granted her.

126 — She would have invented a way to enclose me inside some hermitage, which she would have built on the outskirts of the saint's tomb where the baths were supposedly located.

127 — She would fill the space with flowers and candles, and would even get a traveling musician to play some instrument capable of setting the scene.

128 — She wouldn't allow anyone to touch me.

129 — Anyone to place a finger on my skin.

130 — It would be—following the original nature of the exercise of ceaselessly displaying me—an activity of a purely visual nature.

131 — It occurs to me that it wouldn't have been too much to powder my flesh with a fistful of the diamantine that we use at the Special School to accomplish some chores.

132 — Each week the teacher imposes on us the obligation of doing a manual task, which we must turn in adorned with a layer of brilliant dust.

133 — That is how I began to design homemade lamps, paper ashtrays, bottles of various shapes, whose surfaces were always found covered with the paste that results from mixing the diamantine with the soap foam that, according to the teachers, serves to give real body to objects.

---

134 — Those are some of the few memories that I have of my school years.

135 — Although it is strange, to an extent, to consider events that have just occurred as memories.

136 — Still, although few who believe it are left, I continue to be matriculated here.

137 — It can be said that I am one of the boarders.

138 — That's why I don't understand; if I am someone hindered from going out onto the street, how do I have the time, or, better said, the permission, necessary to spend entire workdays in the baths where my mother dedicates herself to showing me to the rest of the region's women.

139 — The pavilion where I sleep can be considered the biggest in the institution.

140 — While day still hasn't been declared my mother typically enters making as little noise as possible.

141 — To not break the particular silence of those hours, she typically moves in a somewhat strange manner.

142 — She flexes her body in such a way that she transforms it into that of an almost abnormal being.

---

143 — In the baths I have seen bodies similar to those my mother displays when she tries not to make noise many times.

144 — I have noticed that these anomalies may be due to different causes.

145 — I know, for example, that the contact of certain organisms with the environment produces physical alterations difficult to understand.

146 — I am always in relation with bodies exaggeratedly strong and, on the other hand, with skeletons that can barely sustain themselves.

---

147 — Until very recently my mother didn't have, to me, a precise body.

148 — I differentiated her from other women only by the color of her lips.

149 — The only important thing was her besmeared mouth, not the contortions she makes in search of silence.

---

150 — Now, after having gone through so many experiences, I no longer know what to think about my mother's body when I see it enter at night with the key that the director of the Special School seemed to have trusted her with since I was accepted.

151 — It is a long and somewhat rusted key.

152 — Her capacity to enter the pavilion without anyone noticing is astonishing.

153 — Sometimes, although it sounds strange, the effort she makes at contorting her body softly peels the lipstick off her lips.

154 — I never dared to tell her openly, but I like her mouth more when it is presented in that way.

155 — With a somewhat paled sparkle.

---

156 — She almost always waits patiently until she has stretched me entirely out to reapply her lipstick.

157 — On those occasions she gives the impressions doing so with embarrassment.

158 — To undertake the operation she abandons the irregular posture she typically adopts and kneels beside the bed.

159 — But her entrance to the pavilion was not always realized with the most absolute silence.

160 — On more than one opportunity, especially when she had just discovered the potentiality of her lipsticks, my mother stamped her lips over me imbued with a type of frenzy.

161 — Making noises with her throat with such an intensity that I irremediably wound up feeling an erection, which I tried to contain with the skirt of rough material that my own mother has designed for me.

---

162 — Even today I appreciate the consideration that she shows to others when she besmears her lips without anyone noticing.

163 — It would have been terrible had she woken up the rest of the boarders.

164 — It seems she intuits that only by acting in silence can she acquire anything from me.

165 — "How must she get in?" I ask myself each time I see her appear in the darkness.

---

166 — I pointed out that she entered with the key that the school's director had given her.

167 — Nonetheless that supposition seems totally absurd to me.

168 — It is impossible that the director would have given her a key.

169 — For them to let her in perhaps she allots to the groundskeepers some of the objects collected at the baths.

170 — Or perhaps she achieves it by immodestly showing her daubed lips. I imagine that she moves them in such a way that there is no other option but to let her through.

---

171 — Once I wake up completely we leave the pavilion, just as silently.

172 — I am sure that the director doesn't have the slightest idea of our escapes.

173 — I am quite sure that the very strict woman thinks that I sleep entirely through the night in the bed she has assigned to me.

174 — I only see the rest of the boarders when it is time to go to bed, when I return after my daily visits to the baths.

175 — I am also with them on Sundays since on those days my mother, surely to be able to sleep more than usual, is accustomed to leaving me in peace.

176 — I never cease being surprised by her sabbatical laziness.

177 — It is hard for me to believe that she prefers to remain, especially on those days, in her bed instead of collecting even greater numbers of objects than normal.

---

178 — Sundays are truly fruitful days.

179 — Above all at nightfall, when some characters are accustomed to taking, almost hidden, a fortuitous stroll.

180 — They tend to be mostly women who haven't married, or men with varying degrees of femininity, who usually choose the last hours of Sunday to walk the grounds.

---

181 — From time to time they are joined by lovers that have been suddenly abandoned or those afflicted by transmissible diseases—who generally take refuge next to some sewer.

182 — The desperation of many of those present on those days is such that they always arrive weighed down with gifts of the most diverse sources.

183 — They come with bags replete with objects, which I imagine must have taken them many days to gather.

184 — All of this I know because of a memorable Sunday that my mother decided not to spend sleeping.

---

185 — But now, as has been observed, her sleep appears to be indispensable.

---

186 — Before setting course for the baths I usually look on my pavilion companions, sleeping, as if nothing out of the ordinary were happening.

---

187 — "Do they dream?" I ask myself.

---

188 — Not long ago I learned—I think the director herself told me—that I must remain for some time longer a resident of this school.

189 — I no longer miss anything.

190 — I think that with my internment and with the visits to the baths I have more than enough.

191 — It seems to me that neither the memory of my father nor my homesickness for my grandfather's oven are important any longer.

---

192 — I think that my stay here will last the interval of an eternity.

193 — So I will know every corner of its grounds, even the slightest details of the character of its residents, even the deep nature of the teachers' and director's minds.

---

194 — Only now do I realize that at the Special School my testicles don't have any reason to exist.

195 — On those pavilions no one is willing to turn anything over, not to my mother or to me, for the spectacle that they are capable of offering.

196 — Will there be more people interned at the Special School?

197 — Although I do not know it I suspect so.

198 — But I think that I am not unaware of it, I've even affirmed it more than once.

199 — I have always said that I have companions in my reclusion.

200 — I don't have the security, that's true, that many other apparently more important things be true, not just of my present companions but especially in my private life.

201 — I don't know, for example, the number of brothers I have had.

202 — Forgotten, too, my father's face.

203 — Perhaps asking my mother would dissipate my doubts.

204 — But at this point it is absurd to address her directly

205 — It is most likely that she would hide behind one of her lipsticks and show me her face painted with the strangest colors imaginable.

---

206 — After the departure of my father, I never saw anything sensible said to my mother.

207 — Before I was to follow her at all times.

208 — We went together down the streets, through the parks, we passed in front of the houses of those who were accustomed to taking, most of all during the holidays, their pigs to cook in my grandfather's oven.

209 — We took the public buses and more than once we stopped on some corner to drink something.

210 — I accompanied her likewise to do the paperwork at the Special School and, as is known, to our first incursion to the public baths.

---

211 — Only the brilliance of my skin and, of course, the firmness of the bag that contains my testicles makes people think my body stays young.

212 — One time, very early in the morning, I saw, through the window of the pavilion where I sleep, the playground.

213 — The tiny slide, the empty swings.

214 — The sun still hadn't risen.

215 — Almost immediately I felt on my shoulder my mother's hand.

216 — We were late.

217 — I immediately noticed that, on that occasion, she came without the purse that she never wants to separate from.

218 — I saw her without make-up on her face, like in old times, when we lived as a family in a nearby housing estate.

219 — We lived in that place for many years; it was before my mother and I would move to the back house behind my grandfather's oven, where she had spent her childhood and youth.

220 — I remember the housing estate's narrow alleyways, the parking spots for the neighbors' vehicles, the mall.

---

221 — I am never used to transmitting this information.

222 — I don't want to talk about the years that my father, my mother, my brothers, and I formed part of a real family.

223 — Initially the house was rented to us for a couple years; I remember it as a wonderful moment.

224 — With my father, my mother, and my brothers making plans for a better future.

225 — Without yet having the least consciousness of my testicles, at that time so minuscule that I prefer not to refer to them.

---

226 — Once our lease term expired, the landlord began to visit us each night.

227 — He asked us to move out as quickly as possible.

228 — The agreed-to lease had ended, he repeated.

229 — I am not sure, what's more, if my father paid the rent punctually or not.

230 — I do not know if that was an additional reason that the owner contended with his demand.

---

231 — At that time my father was employed at a state agency.

232 — He left the house every day to head to work.

233 — He took a public car, which ran from one side of the city to the other.

234 — The neatness of his white shirts attracted my attention.

235 — Somehow, my mother managed to transfer that brilliance to the skirts that she invented to support my testicles.

236 — But unlike my current underwear, which dirties very quickly because of the constant jostling, my father's shirts resisted dirt for the entire workday.

237 — Once at his office he must have put on some plastic sleeve guards to keep the cloth from deteriorating with his daily routine.

---

238 — There was a period when, here in the baths, my mother refused to accept any type of gift.

239 — I think it happened when she quit utilizing her bag in a normal manner.

240 — She didn't want at that time to receive skirts or bracelets to attach to her wrist.

241 — She began to offer the spectacle of my testicles for free.

242 — It seemed very strange to me that there was no payment.

243 — I didn't like that circumstance.

244 — I was convinced that my genitals should at all times give my mother some kind of satisfaction.

---

245 — This sudden need not to charge arose one dawn, when I interrogated her about her pregnancies when we lived as a family.

246 — When I asked her about the time before we moved to the back house behind my grandfather's oven.

247 — I wanted, like all children, to know if I had had brothers.

248 — But I don't want to speak.

249 — Not about the years that we lived as a family or about the period when we were sheltered in the house behind the oven.

250 — Nor about the reasons why the question about her pregnancies made my mother decide not to accept objects in exchange for my contemplation.

251 — The house, as I noted, had been rented to us for two years.

---

252 — Nonetheless, I insist on affirming that perhaps by questioning my mother many of my doubts would be resolved.

253 — Sometimes I need to know if the contract for the house was really for that period of time.

254 — Although, if I pause and think, I consider it more absurd each time to address her.

255 — Could she really hear someone attentively?

---

256 — More than once have I seen her boast about how young the bag that contains my testicles remains.

257 — She is used to examining it with great care.

258 — Terrified, I imagine, at the possibility of the most minimal symptom of dryness.

---

259 — When my mother examines me I detect in her face certain traces of my grandfather, the one that cooked the pigs.

260 — They say that he died by being chopped into little pieces.

261 — Everything began with a case of diabetes that made them first deprive him of a leg.

262 — My mother always attended to him.

263 — It was an excellent occasion to deny an entire day of her destiny.

264 — At that time she was still single.

265 — Soon thereafter it was necessary to cut off another leg.

266 — Followed by his arms.

267 — My grandfather never stopped staring at an image of Il Duce, Benito Mussolini, on the wall, which he kept at all times as a witness to his experience.

268 — More than once I heard my mother say that my grandfather had in his youth been part of the Urban Brigades.

269 — When that happens, when I begin to imagine traces of our family on my mother's face, I prefer to turn my back to her and look through the pavilion window.

270 — Then I see the playground again.

271 — I stay contemplating the tiny slide, the still swings.

272 — I remain ecstatic until I feel my mother's hand on my shoulder again, which seeks to quickly remove me from my state of contemplation.

---

273 — It is then, having as a background the vision of the abandoned playground, that I remember my testicles' first moments, when they began to form part of my reality.

274 — It was the time when my father's secretary grew gravely ill.

275 — Every afternoon our father sat us at the kitchen table and, while we ate dinner, he gave us a detailed account of the moribund woman's health.

---

276 — "I'm not going to leave the house until they throw us out with a legal eviction," said my father in a convincing manner one evening, when he decided not to talk anymore about his secretary.

277 — It appears that the matter of the eviction from the house was looming.

278 — The visits of the homeowner invited in me a series of feverish states that lasted the rest of the night.

279 — Was it then that I began to be conscious of my genitals?

280 — The fever created images in my head that transformed themselves into a kind of staggering forms.

281 — I think that it was then when I began to imagine that we were in baths situated next to a saint's tomb.

282 — From an unknown faith, what's more.

283 — *Nizamudin, Nizamudin*, I heard more than once in the middle of the darkness.

284 — In moments like this I called out to my mother from my bed, who almost never paid me any attention, busy as she was with attending to her spouse.

285 — I wanted to tell her that I couldn't continue enduring the oppression that such presences caused me, nor the voices that appeared from nowhere.

---

286 — On nights like those I was taken by a sort of premonition.

287 — I saw myself submerged beneath moist surfaces, dragging enormous genitals, and asking several naked men about my father's secretary's health.

288 — That woman was interned in the hospital for many months.

289 — I am sure that those days, when the order of eviction hung over our house, are marked by the sickness that took her to her death.

290 — All the time there were references to complicated dialysis treatments, to indestructible viruses, to the youth and wholeness of the nurse.

---

291 — My mother appeared to be the most affected by the situation.

292 — She looked so upset that during breakfast she wouldn't speak about anything because of the ill-fated woman.

293 — From dawn she would repeat, again and again, that her spouse's lover was condemned to death.

294 — At the time the word lover annoyed me.

295 — Now I don't think it does any longer.

296 — I have even forgotten, here in the baths, its true meaning.

---

297 — Every day, after returning from work, my father gave us a quick recounting of the situation.

298 — My mother listened attentively.

299 — Then she put her hands on her spouse's shoulders.

300 — There she stayed, behind the man that presided over the table.

301 — At remembering them in that way, my insecurity about the real number of family members I had reappears.

302 — I can't remember, most of all, my brothers, to have them present in any of my family scenes.

303 — It would be easy to ask.

304 — But I prefer to remain silent.

305 — It doesn't matter to me any longer to know any additional details about those years.

306 — Although I do desire to preserve the image of those spouses around the table worried about the hospital reports.

---

307 — When my father left the house—he left one morning on his way to his secretary's funeral and did not return—my mother stayed locked inside the house for several months.

308 — Don't think she was fulfilling her habitual routine as a housewife.

309 — She stayed static in one of the kitchen chairs.

310 — Surely without thoughts.

311 — The promised order of eviction, which arrived soon, seemed to rouse her.

312 — A few hours later several men took our things out to the street.

313 — It was strange to observe the beds, the dressers, and the chairs placed in the middle of the sidewalk.

314 — Some neighbors approached.

315 — More than one said that it was the first time that something like that had happened in the housing estate.

316 — My mother was taken to a park by some charitable persons, who sought to keep her a prudential distance from the bustle of those who removed the things from the house.

317 — My brothers—now I understand that I did have brothers—began to hopelessly cry.

318 — Other people, surely more charitable than the first ones, took them to their houses.

---

319 — Before my father's secretary's illness, every once in a while my father sang and played guitar.

320 — On those occasions we gathered in the living room.

321 — The celebrations ceased abruptly.

322 — My father had sung and played the guitar even when the homeowner threatened us with having to leave the house in an instant.

323 — As will be presumed by what I have recounted, the mood took a somber turn.

324 — Some afternoons I saw my mother crying and complaining about the injustice that is a life with invalids.

325 — I never knew who she was referring to: if it was to her own father, if to herself, or if to the moribund secretary.

326 — Now I know that she spoke of me.

327 — That the auguries which by that time she had begun to discern over my person tortured her.

328 — Nonetheless, when I thoroughly consider it, I believe that she exaggerated in her judgements.

329 — That I was not the appropriate person to represent her sadnesses, and am not now either.

---

330 — As we already know, the secretary wound up dead.

331 — My father disappeared forever.

332 — I don't believe my mother can be happy, despite the leather purse that she always carries with her, the colored lipsticks, and the thick bracelets that, from time to time, she wears on her wrists.

333 — For several days a thought, or rather a doubt, has chased me.

334 — I don't know how to tell my mother that soon she will stop receiving the quantity of gifts that she is accustomed to.

335 — I have a premonition that this situation, of displaying my body in exchange for receiving objects, will finish in an instant.

336 — That it will finish, despite the enchantment that the spectacle I am capable of offering continues producing.

337 — Until now everyone seems to consider it impossible that my luminous skin might at some moment decay.

338 — That my testicles might quit looking powerful.

339 — They don't know that I have already begun to experience certain sensations that, sooner or later, will make my genitals turn heavy and smelly.

340 — Precisely because no one suspects it, I have the certitude that the transformation will manifest itself soon.

---

341 — Just as my ancestor, who died by being assassinated by his own mother before she fled to the mountains, must have experienced it, I begin to feel the subtle lengthening of my scrotum.

342 — It seems to follow an invisible guide toward the earth.

343 — Although it happens with the stealth necessary for its decline to take place in the greatest secrecy.

---

344 — When she least expects it it will turn into just a bulge.

345 — At reaching that point I know that my mother won't hesitate a single moment.

346 — She will cut it off with a single slash.

347 — She will then place over the wound a series of substances capable of causing me a rapid infection.

348 — I have no doubt that she will act according to her character.

349 — Surely afterwards she will experience a state of temporary dementia similar to the one my father's abandonment set off, which made her remain seated in a chair for entire days.

350 — She will surely remember the times of my grandfather's pig oven's splendor.

351 — When she was single and ran, with her father, a prosperous business.

352 — The two of them were the only family members to survive the war.

353 — My mother was in charge of decorating the pieces left to cook.

354 — Perhaps in anticipation of that skill she was baptized with the same name as Mussolini's daughter.

355 — She gave them little earrings, diadems, or metal rings, so that each pig being roasted would not be confused with any other.

356 — She will act, I am sure, by wielding the firmness of character with which she tries to convert me into the principal attraction of Saint Nizamudin's tomb, whose outskirts we seem to find ourselves on.

---

357 — Two nights ago my mother brought me some photos that, at first, appeared to just have been taken.

358 — They showed a subject that worked, like my grandfather, the job of a pig roaster.

359 — In the photo I could recognize the walls, the cement tables, the long paddle that my grandfather typically used to complete his work.

360 — I could also see, over their bodies, adornments similar to the ones my mother typically placed on the animals' meat so that it could be recognized by its owners.

361 — They were low-value fantasies, not like the objects that I make with diamantine at the Special School.

362 — My mother and the director always say that my talent isn't anything special.

363 — I haven't heard anything about my father, although surely he more than anyone would have appreciated my lamps covered in soap foam.

The Sheikha's True Illness

CURIOUSLY, THE PROTAGONISTS OF THE LAST BOOK THAT I have published feel satisfied with the work. I think that they come across quite poorly, but they don't seem to notice that they are the characters. I think that they perhaps possess an infinite ingenuity or that they don't usually read books as one should. I arrive at the house where they live and its owner receives me, flanked by the two dogs she owns. They are gigantic hairless specimens. Their backs resemble a mantle of glossy leather. I did not know of that woman's fondness for that type of specimen. When I point it out she is surprised. She adds that, somehow, I had been the driving force behind that interest. It does not cease to be true. It had been more than fifteen years since I had dedicated myself to the promotion of raising dogs of this breed. I have spoken more than once about its benefits. Apart from their intelligence and extreme loyalty, they aren't typically carriers of pests or balls of fuzz that float in the air. They are quite hygienic pets. At seeing clearly the dogs that accompany the woman, I believe I recognize the larger one. It's Lato, the animal that a very close friend's father bought at my insistence five years earlier. It is quite a ferocious beast. It is calm only with whoever is his owner at the moment. With everyone else it is a true beast. Perhaps that is the reason that it has lived in several houses. On a certain occasion, my friend's father had to flee the country in an inopportune departure. At determining that it would be impossible to leave the dog with anyone else, they took it to an animal park, where it escaped from its cage that very night. It then spent more than a week traversing the city from one side to the other, until it could find its original house. No one knows how it managed to orient itself, but despite the great achievement the dog was not welcomed back. The father had already departed and his son, my friend, now alone in the family house, thought that the solution might be to take it to a veterinarian so that they could inject it with some type of poison.

When I learned of the incident, I sought an audience with certain high society women. One of them accepted the dog temporarily. At first the woman had to tolerate a few bites, but the dog quickly seemed to comprehend that being faithful to this new owner was the only way to survive. In its new house, except with its brand new owner, it started to demonstrate extreme fury. It bit every person it met and wanted, what's more, constantly to copulate with its recently acquired owner. After a few months it had to be taken home by some of the house's servants. Faced with the impossibility of tolerating it, the animal was taken to a rural area. There it paid for its faults since, for a reason perhaps related to the food that it began to receive, it began little by little to lose its teeth. Nonetheless, following a series of comings and goings—for economic reasons the rural family had to move to the capital—the dog happened to become the pet of the spouses that I have supposedly portrayed in my last published book.

I recognized the animal fully because it attacked me as soon as it saw me. I remembered, immediately, the matter of the teeth and I held its muzzle, immobilizing its bite. Once the dog calmed down I could continue with my visit. The woman of the house made me come up to the second floor, where her husband was lying on a bed. The woman entered the room first. I stayed at the doorway. From there I saw that the man recognized me and praised not just my last book but my literary career in general. At a certain pause, the wife took the book from the nightstand and asked me how much I charged. I answered her in the way that someone who practices prostitution would and we both laughed. Later, making a gesture entirely in disagreement with the class of person she was, she removed several bills from her cleavage and gave them to me. First she voiced the reservation of not being sure if she had paid me before, when I had launched the book. I did not know if those spouses had been present that night, but I did remember that one of her nieces took a copy, tasked with delivering it to them in the following days.

Once I received the money, the husband suggested that the character in the novel shared his same profession. Then he changed the subject. He talked about the dogs, which had remained on the first floor, since the stairs had a small gate to stop them from coming up. At that moment I told them that on a certain opportunity I had found a specimen of the strange breed's missing link. I added that that gene was still latent, able to spontaneously appear in a generation at the least expected moment. I made that discovery during one of my several trips to the agricultural zones on the coast, where I always ask if they do or don't keep hairless dogs. A villager told me that the fishermen typically owned the smartest specimens. The villager also told me about a phenomenal dog that had been born two years prior. An old woman who dedicated herself to weaving baskets carried it between her hands.

He told me, additionally, that it wasn't the first one to be born in the region. What happened was that the villagers immediately killed the specimens that appeared with those characteristics. The pup had a great hunchback. It lacked a neck and showed great difficulty in moving its head from one side to the other. A particular chronicler of the Indians, Clavijero, mentions a similar specimen called the Izcuintepozoli.

When I finished the story, the husband was already asleep. He was face up with my novel on his chest. The woman had listened to me attentively. Something in her gaze made me suspect that she was worried. The book I had just published began with a similar scene. In the text, while the husband sleeps, his wife wrings her hands in anguish. I stood up—before talking about the Izcuintepozoli I had taken a seat on a small sofa that was in the bedroom—and bade farewell. At descending and opening the little gate to the stairs, the toothless dog tried to attack me. I felt the touch of his gums on my wrist. The wife came down behind me. She accompanied me to the door. The dog continued trying to bite me. The woman continued accusing me. This was no high society woman, as anyone could tell. She was a woman belonging to the Muslim religion. That is why, in the first chapter of the book, I refer to the incongruence that those spouses showed by having hairless dogs instead of salukis, the only canines accepted by Islam. Before closing the door she called me a prostitute; she didn't understand why else I would have sold, to *Playboy* magazine no less, a mystical dream that I had had about the sheikha of the religious community that we belonged to. I was saved, she said, because her husband was ill. That was the reason why he was lying down. She was sure that under those conditions he had been incapable of understanding the reproach, which appeared in the published book, for not having salukis in their home. While she talked she tried to pacify the hairless dog. I never found out if she truly accomplished it. Nonetheless, while I was leaving that home I began to feel a certain embarrassment because, in effect, I had sold, for a high price too, that mystical dream to *Playboy* magazine.

The text had as its title "The Sheikha's Illness," and it is about a few strange visits: first one that I take to the hospital where they treat the incurable illness I suffer from—for which I am considered a sort of martyr for Sufism and am exempt from, among other things, realizing the proper fasting of Ramadan, and another that I take together with our community's sheikha to the house of the plumber charged with fixing the pipes of the mosque where the faithful typically come together several times per week. It seems to me that both visits are important. As much the one to the hospital, where they maintain—in a somewhat artificial manner—my life according to a strict regimen of pills, as the one we make to the house of a plumber for a mosque that strangely doesn't have an appropriate place to perform ritual ablutions. I don't know why I wound up selling the dream to the magazine. Perhaps I did it motivated by the same reasons why in my last published book I portrayed the owners of the hairless dogs in such a pedestrian manner. In no case do the characters come across well. On one hand because the relationship between the owner of the house and the animal leaves much to desire, and even more so the role that the husband plays in that relationship; and on the other for associating my beloved sheikha with a magazine of that nature. I hope that, like the husband of the woman with the dog, my sheikha does not realize that she is a person so portrayed.

The sheikha's illness begins when I appear very upset because I have been treated poorly at the hospital where they attend to me. They have canceled all the appointments I had scheduled, with the labs, with the high prestige doctors, and even a massage session that I managed to get in the rehabilitation area. Almost always those places for physical rehabilitation are located in the basement of the hospital. I know it well because since I was small I have frequently visited them. Since I was born my parents insisted on it in an almost obsessive manner, because I used a prosthesis that replaced my missing right arm. They managed to inculcate in me the need to use it, but they didn't take into account that that type of equipment requires expensive and frequent maintenance. For that reason, for not anticipating that demand and perhaps also because of the lack of economic resources that have always characterized my family, the equipment I have used over the course of my life has always been in worse than calamitous condition. The pieces were imported, super expensive, they seldom had replacement parts. So it was always necessary to make a number of modifications, generally made by traveling cobblers, who did their work the best they could, with which we managed for me to always wear, with the greatest of pride, some useless and unserviceable parody of a prosthesis, which over time didn't do anything but convert me into a type of cripple with half of his chest and right shoulder almost dead. My parents' obsessions were of such magnitude that more than forty years had to pass until, in the middle of a sort of initiating visit to India, I threw my last prosthesis into the sea. I did so two days after the occurrence of the tsunami that devastated part of that country's coast.

But that day, they didn't even want to attend to me in the hospital basement. I must confess that what caused me the most displeasure was the negation of the massage sessions. The rest of the appointments, fundamental to managing my health, didn't bother me much. When I asked for the reasons for their refusing to see me they answered me that they thought that a tragedy had occurred, and that all personnel were on alert to attend to the possible victims. I thought immediately of the tsunami that had happened months earlier. I hadn't been present at the hospitals, but in the airports and in the train stations it was possible to clearly perceive the general bewilderment. That's why, to confirm the reaction that this tragedy would now inspire, I made the decision to leave through the emergency room door. Curiously, I didn't notice anything out of the ordinary. I went past the tiny doctors' offices in that area and in front of the waiting room without encountering any major setbacks. There were, seated in their chairs, those suffering from urgent ailments. Nonetheless, they didn't surpass the normal number of patients. It seemed to be about the number of afflicted they were used to.

Despite all prognostics, when I was at the point of leaving that area I suddenly ran into the sheikha. She was being transported, with great speed, in a wheelchair. Duja, one of our dervishes, was pushing her. A tall, imposing woman with a privileged voice. Her personal servant accompanied them. I approached them, and greeted them with the traditional *As-salamu alaykum*, but I did not receive an answer. They passed me as if I did not exist. Duja, with her characteristic voice, asked for a doctor. I knew that the doctors were not available. That because of the general emergency they were not attending to anyone as was supposed to be their custom. I then remembered that as I was a regular patient, I knew the nooks and crannies of the hospital and could easily find one of my favorite doctors.

I ran into the hospital. I went down certain hallways. I went up staircases. I took elevators. I had great difficulty walking among the patients and their relatives, who were used to moving from one section to another, totally occupying the access routes. I remembered the suggestion that I had considered formulating several months ago. Of creating a type of rules-for-moving so that the people would properly circulate inside the hospital. Most of all for the stairs, since it was torture to have to go up and down them at the time of the highest flow of patients. As I intuited, I found one of my doctors in a small research room. I looked through a minuscule round window in the middle of the door, and I saw him working in front of a microscope. I opened the door without knocking and, curiously, the interruption didn't seem to affect him. He left what he was doing and gestured toward a place for me to sit. He must have thought that I wanted him to examine me. I had the temptation to tell him that I had in fact had an appointment with him, which had been canceled because that day the hospital's order had been altered. But I remembered the case of the sheikha. At that moment my health didn't matter. I asked him to accompany me. He seemed willing to do so, but first he asked me what a sheikha was. I had to explain to him that it was the spiritual leader of the Sufi community that I belong to. I added that she was poor of health. That Duja, our singing dervish, had taken her to the emergency room with the intention of curing the ill she was suffering.

The doctor left his tasks to one side and exited behind me. Our mission was so important that I didn't make any comment about the slowness of the patients and their relatives obstructing the hallways. Neither did I ask what the emergency was that had thrown the hospital's appointments out of order. I would have wanted to ask many more things. Matters of genetics most of all. To talk to him about the hairless dogs. About the missing links that it is still possible to find in the fishing villages. About the famous Izcuintepozoli. But I didn't do it. Like I also didn't ask him if he had read the last books I had published, which I gave him as gifts after each consultation. The important thing was to get through that sea of sick people and arrive at the emergency room. We managed it after several long minutes. At entering the hallway I could make out the sheikha, Duja, and her servant. They were in a similar position to when I had left them. The doctor approached them and told them to wait. He would go to find an adequate room, he indicated. I looked at the sheikha's face. She continued to show signs of being in pain. It was no longer Duja that held the wheelchair. The servant now held on to it.

Despite being in front of her, the sheikha didn't seem to recognize me. She looked withdrawn into her pain. At the same time Duja began to direct herself at me with naturalness, but she didn't tell me the condition that the sheikha was in. Where she had found her. How bad she was suffering. The only thing that I managed to hear is that she begged God that she would be promptly attended to. When the doctor returned, he said that he hadn't found a room adequate to auscultate a sheikha. Therefore he needed to check her over in a garden. They had already taken the necessary precautions. I couldn't understand then how, in the midst of such disorder, at that hospital they had been able to take the necessary measures for the revision of a person of such characteristics so quickly. But in effect, several minutes later we found ourselves in an interior garden—I think it was one that was located inside the offices of the director—with some of the personnel ready to begin their work. They had installed a table over the grass, and the doctor was accompanied by two nurses. They made Duja, the servant, and me wait in a corner, next to a rosebush. From there we saw how they lifted the sheikha from her chair and placed her on the table. It was at that moment that I noticed the shoes that the sheikha wore. They were a model that I had never seen before. They were made of black velvet and they featured a series of complicated straps that tied to her ankles. At the end of each strap there were pompoms of a lighter black, like a crow's wing.

The doctor and the nurse began the work of trying to untie the shoes. The task started becoming more and more complicated. At that moment Duja's servant spoke. She asked how it was possible for them to attempt to undertake such a job. That very few met the requisite conditions to remove a sheikha's shoes. She added that none of those present could do so. I felt a great shame. I had made the doctor I was most confident in come—on that special day, with an imminent tragedy threatening us—to the garden. I had made them install the table, as it should be available to auscultate a sheikha, and because of the issue of some shoes that couldn't be untied everything was being thrown off track. But the servant was implacable. From the most absolute immobility she kept repeating, again and again, that none of those present were within their rights to remove a sheikha's shoes. Without our noticing, Duja began to stealthily leave the garden. I noticed it because of a soft canticle that she emitted while she distanced herself. It seemed to me, I don't know why, that her steps were similar to those stepped by the old lady who made baskets in the fishermen's port I visited from time to time.

Meanwhile, the doctor and the nurses seemed not to hear the servant's words and continued with their fruitless labor. They wanted to remove the sheikha's shoes however they could. To see her lying on the table while her shoes were being manipulated reminded me of a similar scene that took place on the street, very near the mosque, weeks ago. On that occasion one of our most beloved dervishes, Cherifa, an older woman, had been run over by a vehicle when she went out to buy the tea that we faithful who had gathered to pray that night would drink. Our sister was lying in the middle of the street, and some neighbors had covered her in newspaper. It was raining. In the mosque the gathered faithful had no idea of what was happening outside. They were concentrated on their evening prayer, while Cherifa struggled in pain and loneliness. That same day I had had a dream about Cherifa. In some way the elements that would later be unleashed were all present. Cherifa was seated on a bus—the same one that would later run her over—in the company of her daughter-in-law, Rajmana. Both seemed content with the trip. I found myself seated two rows further back. I was accompanying the woman who owned the hairless dogs. We went on the trip with just one of the animals, the more fierce one, the one that escaped from the animal park where they wanted to confine it and ran kilometers and kilometers until finding its house again, where my best friend, to rid himself of it, thought first of injecting it with poison. It was a perfect dog. As is known, of a disobedient and aggressive character, but its shape was ideal. On the bus it was very annoying. it wanted to copulate with the woman that accompanied me, who seemed incapable of controlling it. Strangely, on that occasion the dog didn't manage to bite me. I don't remember if at that time it had his complete set of teeth. I suspect that it didn't since it had already been returned to me by the family of servants. This was dreamed during the early morning of the eleventh of August of the year 2005, the accident occurred during the evening of the eleventh of August of the same year. Happily the damages caused to Cherifa's body weren't more severe. Neither, it seems, was the suffering she endured in the street's solitude. She was stunned, thrown to the ground, accompanied by some policemen and some neighbors, to whom nothing occurred but to cover her body with old newspapers.

But the sheikha remained laid out. The straps of her shoes couldn't be removed an iota. I would have liked to have known what the husband of the woman that owned the hairless dogs, who comes across so poorly in the last book that I have published, would have thought of the situation—of the sheikha lying on a wood table waiting to have her shoes removed. That man who, without noticing that he and his wife are the characters depicted, slept with my book on top of him after his wife gave me, as if I were just anybody, some bills that she took out from her cleavage. I haven't mentioned it, but at receiving that money I felt, in some way, like when I was a child and pretended on the phone to be an indigenous woman looking for work as a servant. I remember that I was ten or eleven years old, and, in hiding, looked through the newspaper classifieds to make calls imitating the lexicon of women from the interior. They almost always wound up making me sexual propositions, which I accepted over the telephone with the greatest of pleasure.

I don't know exactly why I remembered those calls when I heard the whisper of Duja leaving through the hospital garden. It was an ignorance similar to that which made me not know why I had associated her stealthy steps, distancing themselves amidst canticles, with those of the Izcuintepozoli puppy's old owner. Surely Duja in those moments would be leaving through the same emergency room door where she entered, pushing the wheelchair. Perhaps the servant that she left with me was the personification of my childhood telephone games. But in this case she didn't seem to fulfill any sexual function, and instead limited herself to repeating the litany of the impossibility of taking off a sheikha's shoes. A sheikha lying down in one of the internal gardens of the hospital where they supposedly keep me alive, where I received my medical reports and endured a number of sufferings before an adequate medicine would be found capable of discarding my illness into some sort of infinity prescribed by medical science. "You will die of anything but your disease," they have repeated to me an infinity of times. I should believe it, although at times there are medical errors that make it impossible for one to blindly accept its precepts. From there the preoccupation that they would rapidly attend to the sheikha's illness. The dreams I've experienced during my Sufi trances don't always have happy results. Not all prophecies were limited to Cherifa's horror, almost unconscious and lying in a street in the middle of the rain surrounded by policemen and by neighbors disposed to cover her body with sheets of newspaper. That horror ended precisely when Duja, our dervish who had a privileged voice, arrived that evening late to prayer and encountered the spectacle. After delivering to Cherifa, who still had no clear idea of what was happening, some words of consolation she went to the mosque, where she interrupted the prayers with the news.

Within the prophecy dreams of death also exist. Therefore the urgency to remove the sheikha's shoes as soon as possible. At that other moment, in the dream of death, I see that an unknown doctor is checking me over, not the one attempting to treat the sheikha. It is another doctor, who looks at my face with circumspection; he seems amazed by certain cutaneous deformations. He explains that he must analyze them. It turns out that the possibility exists that they are malignant manifestations. I remember the affair of the neck. Of the putrid neck that attacks me from time to time. The doctor agrees. To present every so often with a putrid neck can be a signal that the results are positive. He tells me that there are three stages to reach. In the worst, which he suspects, I will die within five years. I am bothered. It seems like a very distant date. Let me live or let me die, I insist. If this stage is supposedly the most severe one, let me die immediately, not in five long years.

Soon, within that dream of death, I find myself inside a car, taking a person to the emergency room of some sanatorium. I don't know who it is. They have a certain resemblance to the character that I portray in my last published book. They also resembled the technician who designed my prosthesis for me in the basement of the hospital of my childhood. I suppose that it must be a similar trance to the one that Duja, our dervish, has had to endure, to hurriedly transport the sheikha. Perhaps to make the process more practical. To lift and lower the sheikha, call the nurses, or to assemble and disassemble the wheelchair she decided to take the servant with her. That morning a fellow Sufi, Nuh, died, afflicted with the AIDS virus. I try to find some relation. There are now too many embarrassing elements. The characters from the last book that I've published, the hairless dogs, the father of my friend abandoning his favorite animal for motives of travel, my friend—as will be seen further on, because of a prophecy he fell backward from the choir to the central nave of a village church. The presence of the lost link in the hairless dogs. The absence of canines of the saluki breed, the only ones approved of by Islam. The sheikha's illness. The accidents of everyday life.

At Nuh's wake, with the coffin covered in a green sheet that provides the illusion that there is no coffin beneath it, I pause to think when I see the total display of the whirling dervishes dancing, whirling unto infinity. Before the body? I then make plans for the manner of elimination of my own body. I want as soon as possible to sign a letter that appoints the sheikha so that the families can't intervene in the dervishes' final decision. To be kept vigil over and buried according to the Muslim ritual. There are economic problems with this matter, above all because for many members of the community it is impossible to have the money necessary to not be cremated. One of my dreams is to convert a fully forested lot I bought some years ago—which is now abandoned because of a set of problems as much of a legal as of a personal nature—into a Sufi cemetery. I don't dare propose it. Perhaps I am not sure of my faith. I have heard many times that the Sacred Koran places the cloth of judgment first upon he who in some way believes it. It says that those who believe falsely—in other words, all Muslims at some point in their lives—will be those most severely punished.

"The eye should be the size of what it perceives," I heard the sheikha say more than once. I never dared to ask what it was that that meant. What I did understand in a clearer way was when she told us that when the human being loves something he only loves the human being—he loves himself, his own attributes reflected in that which he says he loves. And I love the sheikha, my spiritual leader. That is why I cannot permit her to remain lying down without their being able to untie the laces to her shoes. I try to intervene. I hush the servant, who continues repeating her litany, and address the doctor directly. At hearing me, he gives an order to the nurses to stop trying to untie the tassels and straps that fasten the black velvet shoes. Then he looks at his watch. It is the end of shift, he announces. Better for everyone, he continues. This hospital isn't prepared to receive a sick sheikha. The patient must be taken to another branch. Just the servant and I remain responsible for the patient. We must sign some forms, the doctor tells us, to take responsibility for such a decision. I ask the servant how they have arrived at the hospital. The servant responds that they arrived in the sheikha's car. It can't be, I respond, disconcerted.

The sheikha is the owner of a useless '67 Datsun. It is impossible for us to take responsibility for the transfer in such an unsafe vehicle. I remember that one time I saw the sheikha driving it downtown, at a minimal speed furthermore. At that moment it became clear to me that the sheikha, to me, was no more than a species of transit between one instance and another. That is to say, that she served me as a reference point to be sure of the existence as much of a material world as of one formed only of the spirit. Although surely she would not have been in agreement with my form of thinking, because she had insisted again and again that everything was one and the same. Despite herself, the presence of the sheikha permitted me not to confuse one with the other. Perhaps for this reason, for having so limited my perception of reality,

I didn't always feel like a true dervish. Doubt attacked me at certain stages. Sometimes, as on this occasion, I was taken by the two opposite feelings at the same time. That is why when I saw the car disappear in the city's traffic, I missed my visits to the mosque and, nonetheless, had no urge whatsoever to visit it. I think that that rejection lasted until Nuh's death—like me, another martyr of Sufism. The morning of her departure, when I remained asleep for the length of a day, I saw that a doctor, who I repeat was not one of those who attend to me regularly, talked to me about the three stages. Each one contradictory to the others. Despite bringing airs of death, the three are encouraging in a certain sense. "...once the power of the soul is reached," I heard the doctor say to me as his last words before disappearing. I know that that morning I dreamed of the disappearance—that is, of Nuh's death. Immediately on getting out of bed I got on the internet, and found the email from the sheikha convoking the funeral rites.

Getting into a Datsun like the sheikha's can have many consequences. I know. That is why I am doubting. I have the papers before me. To the surprise of all, at that moment the sheikha seems to resuscitate. The color has returned to her face. She sits up on her own strength and asks that they leave her shoes in peace. She immediately understands the situation and says that she will sign to take responsibility for herself. She sits up without anyone's help. Her elasticity surprises me. In the mosque she always asks for assistance to sit up. On more than one occasion I have thought that she solicits that help in deference to others. So that the dervishes are satisfied that that night they helped a sheikha get up. The sensation that comes over me at seeing the sudden change of the situation's tone is similar to that which I experienced when Hazim—a person that I don't know but whom I nonetheless always feel very close with—and I made a sort of pilgrimage, circling and circling around an important mosque. It is very long building, with high red walls. It shares similarities with the great mosque that I visited in India shortly before separating myself from the prosthetic apparatus that had tortured me since childhood. From the apparatus that atrophied my shoulder and part of my chest. There is a great quantity of parcels of land around it, organized according to the colors of the products that are harvested. In front of these colors each pilgrim had to pause to make an offering. Hazim and I walked very close together. The fear that the illness he suffered from—evidenced in an extreme skinniness—produced in me was evident. But that pilgrimage around the mosque we had no intention of entering gave us a certain relief, as much from his illness as from mine.

Bismilah id rajmani rajím, we heard rising always from inside. Sufism posits that we have completely forgotten the ideal world we come from. The voices that came out of the mosque told us that our labor is in remembering, in remembrance. The heart must remember, remember its entire previous life. Still, at that moment I could only remember the fact that my childhood friend wanted to poison the dog after the animal gave a thorough display of faithfulness. After traversing the entire city and arriving to scratch at the door of the house, that dog was sent to have a dose of poison administered. It is true that his father had departed. That there was no one in the house to take responsibility for the animal. But such a measure is cruel, no matter how it seems. Perhaps that's why that friend, years later, suffered the punishment of falling backwards from the choir of a village church.

On that occasion we had decided, with three other friends, to cross the border between Mexico and the United States. One of the friends who was going with us offered to serve as our guide. We joked about the fences. My friend knew the way to cross from one side to the other without anyone noticing. Once we were dozens of kilometers across—we traveled in a specially equipped van—we noticed that the Mexican spirit remained in some way present. In that instant we knew that our friend, the guide, had been a real human trafficker. We stopped the van and told her so. Our friend seemed offended. We had stopped in a very old, tiny town, which had no relationship with the nearby villages. It had a typical church. We left our friend in the van. The rest of us entered the temple to visit. My friend, the one that had tried to poison his father's hairless dog, climbed up into the choir, which was very high. Without noticing, he took a step backwards and fell to the center of the nave. We approached him and confirmed that he was dead. I recall. The scene is absurd. Primarily because I am not sure if my friend climbed up to the choir. In that case the scene is beyond absurd. To fall he would have first had to have climbed up. Still, my friend was dead. Supposedly, soon thereafter, in that village, a tragedy of significant proportions would occur. That was the complete prophecy. If my friend fell from the choir the tragedy would engulf that place. Something similar to the tsunami that affected India when I was visiting. In some way, what my friend's death seemed to be trying to say was that he had died to avoid a greater death. No one knows anything. The only truth is that our friend was dead and not the hairless dog, which is now property of the protagonists of my last published book, who, curiously, feel satisfied with the work. The woman of the house surrounded by dogs, her husband with my book open on his chest. The fiercest dog without a single tooth in its mouth. Still, I can't focus on anything but Duja's traversing, after subtlety abandoning us, as if she were fleeing some source of guilt, the streets of the city.

The sheikha, once she stands up, asks the servant for the keys to her Datsun, which she wants to drive to the indicated hospital branch. The servant hands them over to her. She places them on one side of the wooden table. The sheikha is now standing. She walks to the parking lot. She rejects the wheelchair that I offer her. The doctor and the nurses are overcome with courtesies before such a particular patient. I take advantage of the occasion to complain about the bad treatment that I have received that morning at that hospital. I recount, one by one, the canceled appointments, the failed drawings of blood, and most importantly, the abbreviated massage sessions I was going to be treated to in the basement. I say that I am tired of being discriminated against. In no sector of society, save at that center, do I endure such treatment. I think, and I say it aloud, that that is perhaps because my writing has served as a sort of prophecy of what would later happen in my life. I don't mention it as much for the description of the hospital's basement, present when I published my first book in 1983, *The Women of Salt*, nor for my friend's falling death, but for the construction and development of the *Moridero*, a fundamental piece of my book *Beauty Salon*.

Scared at such a terrible diagnosis, when they told me the illness that I suffered from, I went to seek refuge at a doctor's, an acquaintance of the sheikha's, who owned a type of clinic, which turned out to be a real-life portrait of what ten years earlier had been conceived of in that book as the *Moridero*. And it was not only the physical space that left me stupefied, but that the personality of that crazed and cruel doctor, who was an imposter in the worst sense, is portrayed as a character in the text of *Beauty Salon*. Writing as prophecy. It is not in vain that in the Islamic religion the miracle is a book and we are just a letter in that book. That is perhaps the reason, being simply a letter in an infinite book, why when a practitioner of Sufism boards a plane or train they usually go through a number of experiences somewhat outside the ordinary. Generally, when they are at the point of boarding some mode of transportation, they feel the unusual impulse of selecting, from among the group of unknown people that typically populate the gates at airports, some person whom they would never in life like to detach from. Like a letter that seeks to stick to another letter to form a word.

Something tells them that the person in front of them will form, from then on, a fundamental part of their existences. But, despite such a curious circumstance, they can't abandon the scheduled trip. Feelings must be suppressed and they must act like a common and everyday person. They have done quite enough already to travel, having removed the robes with which they customarily pray, or the attire necessary to effect the mystical whirls, the same outfits, so determined in their configuration, that I observed during Nuh's ceremony of farewell, in front of her casket covered with a sheet of green cloth.

By the way, what clothes would Cherifa have been wearing when she was run over? Everything would indicate that it would have been her prayer robe. Before the accident occurred she was already partaking in the ceremony. What would be logical would be for her to have remained in the mosque all night. But, suddenly, someone noticed that the tea that was traditionally offered to the faithful was lacking. Certainly at that moment Cherifa was already facing toward Mecca to begin her prostrations. But instead of beginning her prayer she offered to go to the store. That's how minutes later she wound up splayed out on the pavement, run over, with the neighbors covering her robe with some sheets of newspaper. Since that accident, our sheikha has determined that once they've entered, no one leaves the mosque. They must wait until the night ends to do so. That assures that within the mosque one is absolutely unprotected, undressed, with the senses tuned for spiritual practice and not for facing the everyday world. On what plane of reality would Cherifa find herself at the moment of the accident? Perhaps on the same one where the members of Sufi communities typically find themselves at train stations or airports before boarding some mode of transportation. Before directing themselves to the boarding zones they are accustomed to making the oath that, despite their bodies' displacement by hundreds of miles, they will not cease from remaining next to the person selected moments before. For some, the intention to take the memory of the beloved, unknown person, with them for many hours could represent the staging of an extremely romantic scene. To others a simple manifestation of schizophrenia. Rather, it is, I think, the search that any member of a community of this nature must undertake to be present in the spirits of several people at the same time. To form complete words. During the trip, while remaining in their assigned place, they are typically awed by the sensation that causes them to notice that they are capable of displacing their bodies by unimaginable distances and, at the same time, remain static at the point where they found the person that they selected to never separate from. I am not sure if the sheikha has knowledge of the practice that many of her disciples undertake before traveling. I don't think that such an activity would produce any enthusiasm in her. The sheikha has seen many miracles in her life. One of them was that they would choose her, at her age, as the sheikha of the community that she directs. Her interest seems only to be the aspects of divine grandeur. Although, as will be seen further ahead, I attempted to find this display in the most banal actions.

While she walks, the sheikha appears to feel better and better. She is no longer even the shadow of the sick woman that entered the hospital's emergency room. She says that she, as is customary, will drive her Datsun. It was already more than enough for Duja to have driven her to the hospital. I remembered then that I had always driven my own car. Until before they had stolen it from me, at gunpoint, in one of the city's most central zones. I also liked to drive my own car when I visited the rural zones on the country's coast, where I discovered that the most intelligent specimens of hairless dogs were owned by the fishermen. I think that my interest in those landscapes was born in the memory of the trips I took with my father, a technician of agricultural affairs, to similar zones. I remember from those times the parcels of land separated according to the products that would be harvested. Still, the colors of those parcels were not as luminous as those I saw each time I pilgrimaged around the mosques with Hazim, my sick friend. The sheikha surely intuits that if I drive the Datsun we will never arrive at our destination. I try to remember some occasion when I have driven in her presence. Only the afternoon when I took them, the sheikha and her mother, from the mosque to the house that they inhabited appears. I remember that it was a fun trip. Her mother seemed to overly enjoy the sports car that I owned at that time. She liked its color and the roof, which opened automatically. But there was another occasion when I tried to serve as a guide to the sheikha while she was driving her own Datsun. It was when she did me the favor of accompanying me, for the first time, to the hospital where I encountered her. The image appears at the moment when we were returning from the appointment. We had already seen the doctor, who had given his verdict. We were disoriented by a series of dark streets that seemed to lead to nowhere. We quit being lost when the sheikha stopped the car and affirmed that, from that moment, I passed into the category of Sufi martyr. Years earlier, she had asked the supreme guide of the Sufis, Muzafer Efendi, who lived in Turkey, about the details—about what happened to the dervishes that were condemned to death. Immediately, there in the car, there appeared in my head the plastic image of the small whirling dervish that is located on a ledge in the mosque. The little statue had lost an arm several months ago. I asked myself if that type of dervish would also belong to the category of martyr. I also asked myself if Duja, with her physical characteristics, was also a martyr of Sufism. Or if the sheikha herself, ill and imprisoned in some black velvet shoes, was also one. Perhaps her mother, who enjoyed my car roof opening mechanically, like a little girl, would indeed belong to a similar category.

Although I think that the only martyr present in this text is my childhood friend, lying dead after falling from the church choir. It was not possible for that to happen. Outside, in the van that transported us, was the guide who had oriented us to cross the border in a clandestine manner. She sniveled because we had accused her, as is known, of being a human trafficker. How could she grieve about that when such a tragedy had occurred inside the church? We had to abandon the town however we could. To load everyone into the specially equipped van and flee as quickly as possible. We had to leave the cadaver lying in the central nave. To abandon him in the same way as his father had left the country. I don't want to think about what would have happened in that house after the father's leaving if, in the place of the dog that they owned they had had a specimen of the missing link, the Izcuintepozole. Certainly the father would have killed it when he left. At the moment of making the decision to leave the country, he wouldn't have had any alternative to making it disappear. It was impossible to undertake the work of taking that monster to the animal park. There perhaps they would have recommended a museum to exhibit it stuffed. It was clear that the hairless dogs suffered greatly at the act of being caged. Perhaps that was the reason why my friend's father's specimen, named Lato, fled on the same day of its abandonment. Surely it took a great leap out and joined some visitor. Perhaps it pretended to be a companion dog and, stealthily, with a care even greater than that which Duja displayed when she abandoned the sheikha in the hospital garden, escaped to the street.

Our guide, who at noticing what was happening suddenly quit crying, recommended that the best thing to do would be to return to Mexican territory. We should take refuge from the great tragedy in that country. In that moment we couldn't have known it was going to have to do with an earthquake, with a tornado, or with a flood.

The only thing that we knew was that we had to flee. So she began to drive the van in a fast manner. Nonetheless, a few tears still escaped her. She no longer cried because of our accusation from a few moments earlier. Now she did, finally, for my dead friend. Nonetheless, despite the vehicle's speeding up she drove well. The sheikha of the Sufi community that I belong to does so in the same way. A little slow, that's true, but with impeccable dexterity. When I muster my last attempt to tell her, at the door of the hospital, that in her physical condition she should turn over the steering wheel, she tells me the disconcerting phrase that no one trips twice on the same stone. I keep thinking about that sentence. I realize then that my spiritual leader doesn't have the least confidence in me. I look at her carefully. She seems to feel better with each moment. The car, as I noticed at the moment, is a pile of junk that can barely run. That is why at our passing a series of traffic incidents begin to be produced, provoked mostly by the incredibly low velocity that we begin to move at. I must acknowledge that I don't have the slightest idea of the route that we're taking. At that moment I realize that I have never had any idea how to arrive at the hospital branch where we're headed. I had told the sheikha to drive. I had even been at the point of signing the letter establishing my responsibility for her, but I had ultimately ignored what was being asked of me.

Only in that instant did I give the sheikha a reason to deny me the steering wheel. Again I noticed what we dervishes always know, but which we often let pass over our heads. That a sheikha never makes a mistake, and that many times her apparently erroneous actions are no more than the disguise of a lesson that we are not always prepared to receive. The journey seems long. I ask myself then what the temporal afflictions that tend to attack sheikhas could consist of. I think that they might have to do with hidden precepts, but I intuit that most of the time those afflictions symbolize things of greater complexity. To demonstrate that there is no God but God, for example, or that reality is all one thing. In a foolish manner, since on many occasions I refuse to accept the extranatural quality of spiritual leaders, I wanted to know if the afflictions, when they trouble them, are real illnesses or fleeting circumstances. On some occasions I have a feeling that those diseases have their origins in a set of images thattend to overtake them, precipitately, especially during the morning prayers. I quickly disposed of those lucubrations. I intuited that I created them to leave aside my principal preoccupation. To have published, in *Playboy* magazine no less, a story based on a mystic dream: "The Sheikha's Illness." That had to be the principal reason for my affliction and my guilt.

I believe that the high society Muslim woman's yelling at me that I was a simple prostitute helped me recognize that I had been mistaken. I ran, that same night, toward the door of the mosque. I didn't even think of first passing by their niece's house, who despite her promises to do so never came to pay for the book that she took on the day of the presentation. I arrived at night. It was early. The street was empty. From where I found myself I could perfectly make out the corner where Cherifa had been run over. I waited several hours. Although it was a day when the brethren met, I didn't notice anyone entering or leaving that house of prayer. Time passed. I don't remember when the doors—not the doors of the mosque but those of the institute of religious studies, which is located on the second floor—opened. The sheikha exited through that door accompanied by Nadira, another dervish sister with whom she has a strained intimate relationship. The two have left for just a few moments. They tell me so when I greet them. They are going to return one hour later, they confirm. I tell them that I want to deliver the hundreds of *tasbis*—rosaries—for prayer that I bought wholesale during my trip to India to the mosque that same night. I have them packaged at home, but I can quickly go for them. The beads are made of wood and the *tasbis* are packaged by the dozen. Nonetheless, neither the sheikha nor Nadira seem to display interest in this matter. It seems strange to me, because in one of our meetings the sheikha complained that the community didn't have enough *tasbis* to entrust them to the new faithful during their baptismal ceremonies. A green car waits for them at the door. I note that it's the same color as the sheet they cover Nuh's casket with on the day of her farewell. Before they get in it, Nadira directly approaches where I am standing. She is furious. I had not noticed earlier, but she's burning holes with her eyes. She tells me that she finds herself extremely upset with me. I suspect that she has discovered that the sheikha has appeared in the pages of *Playboy* magazine. Only then do I realize that the sheikha has not responded to any of the emails that I sent her from Europe, where I traveled to deliver a series of conferences about my work. Neither had she accepted, before undertaking a trip of that nature, to make an appointment to say goodbye. I had wanted to organize a dinner at my house or to invite her to a restaurant. It had all been useless. I had wanted for us to talk deeply about the sort of pilgrimage that I was going to undertake. After the conferences in Europe I would go to India, to visit the tombs of some saints. But the two women, before getting into the green car, instead of addressing my offering of the *tasbis*, told me to continue waiting at the door. They would be back before long, they repeated. When I followed the car while it was shifting into gear, I seemed to perceive a certain alcoholic aroma on the sheikha's breath. I was surprised. Later I learned that in Sufi communities the drunkenness of the soul is the ultimate state one can reach. "Each human being is a transcription of *the* being, and for that reason is inherently perfect," the sheikha rattled on. Nadira was still upset. She asked the sheikha not to continue delivering the word to me.

I soon stopped. I was somewhat agitated. I hadn't even run a half block but I was out of breath. I asked myself at that moment if that phrase, the one the sheikha said through the window, had any bearing on my dead friend. I never learned what happened to his splayed body. If he remained in the middle of the nave forever, or if he found himself beneath hundreds of tons of mud. The situation led me to a set of somewhat exotic teachings, which were imparted by the school of Ahmed Jalali, a master with extreme ideas about love. Ahmed Jalali said, for example, that love is not an attribute of God because it is God itself. I never asked the sheikha what she thought of that point of view. I would have liked to have asked it when I needed to understand the conduct of my friend's father, who abandoned his dog at an animal park. Or that of my own friend, who tried to poison it just because. To ask if it was feasible to pray for the driver of the bus that ran over Cherifa. Or to lift our prayer for Duja, who distanced herself from the hospital garden, walking backwards and singing under her breath. I think that the best thing would have been to pray for our dervish brethren, who in different transit stations decide to select an anonymous person whom they will never detach from again for as long as they live. Brethren who, regardless of the physical place where they find themselves, will be at the same time and in every place together with the chosen soul.

"There is no God but God," I heard the sheikha explaining in the Datsun to Duja's servant, who had followed us from the garden and was seated in the backseat. The journey seemed longer and longer. The monotony was only interrupted by some commentary by the sheikha, who besides trying to explain matters of faith to the servant—*lailahailaláh, Mohammed rasulalá*—made annotations referring to the ramshackle car and to the city's intense traffic. At a certain moment she turned her head and told the servant that I was her best dervish. Those words impressed me. Among other things, I thought of what terrible dervishes the rest must be. I then felt a sort of nostalgia for the community that I belong to. In that instant the car stopped in front of a small house. Still, this didn't seem to matter to me. I continued listening to the words that the sheikha was pronouncing. Soon

I seemed to see Fariha, the sheikha from the New York community, leaving through the door. I didn't at that moment have any way to know that it was the house of the plumber that would make some repairs to the mosque's pipes. The sheikha had deceived us all. My trusted doctor, the nurses, the servant and me. She could not lie to Duja, so our singing dervish had stealthily left the garden where she was placed on the wooden table. At no moment was the sheikha heading in her Datsun to the hospital branch. She knew from the beginning, before anything, that the mosque's drainage system needed repair. She had knowledge, additionally, that we faithful needed basins to devote ourselves to our ablutions with the utmost comfort.

As I don't understand the situation, that we are in reality in front of the plumber's house, I consider Sheikha Fariha's leaving that little house the most normal thing in the world. I think that perhaps she has rented it to spend a season in Mexico. Sheikha Fariha, draped in lavish skirts and glass beads, tells me when she sees me that the next Ramadan will bring me a saluki, Islam's preferred canine. She repeats that Ramadan will bring it to me, not her herself. I don't believe her. I think that Sheikha Fariha will do everything possible to acquire me one. I suppose that it will be a saluki puppy. Not a dog of adult age. I imagine that in New York there are specialized breeders. As many must know, the saluki is the dog of the desert Bedouins. It is a sand dog, a hunter par excellence. A sand dog that doesn't dig up the dead with its claws. That is why it was the only one accepted by the followers of the Prophet Mohammed—peace be upon him—because other varieties of canines tried to profane his tomb. It is the reason why the companions of the Prophet—peace be upon him—mandated that every dog that existed from Mecca to Medina be eliminated. The salukis were the only ones that escaped the mandate. Curiously, despite having been in their moment the only surviving variety, today they are almost impossible to find. Generally, to do so, to locate an authentic one, one must carry out long voyages across the desert. Mostly fruitless searches, since a Bedouin very rarely lets go of one of his specimens. They are dogs as rare as the Izcuintepozoli, which it seems that no divine blessing capable of preserving them fell upon. For me the only image that remains of that missing link is that featuring the old basket weaver walking, with steps very similar to Duja's as she left the garden, with her creature between her hands. Nonetheless I come to trust in Sheikha Fariha, who suddenly left the plumber's house as if it were hers. I repeat, Sheikha Fariha, draped in lavish skirts and glass beads, tells me on seeing me that the next Ramadan will bring with it a saluki for me.

She tells me again that Ramadan will bring it for me, not her herself. To wait with longing and joy for Ramadan. Not to fear those dates. That I have suffered plenty. That from now on good fortune awaits me. That it will begin with the arrival of the dog that is not a dog.

Despite having seen her exit from that house, it didn't have anything to do, even distantly, with a property rented by Sheikha Fariha. In the front there was a set of abandoned car frames. Also the remains of tubing and construction supplies. To my surprise—as I still thought we were headed to the hospital branch indicated by the doctor—the sheikha said that we were at the house of the plumber who would make the repairs to the pipework at our mosque. Confirming the supposed deceit made me recall how devastated my favorite dervish Malika and I once were because it was the end of the year and they hadn't scheduled any meetings at the mosque. We found ourselves in the apartment of an almost unknown Muslim brother, he was a Sunni that we had encountered through strange circumstances, who very kindly invited us to his house where he laid out rugs to make prayer, which we rigorously did, but still we felt devastated. The truth was that with that Sunni—which, as is known, is a branch of Islam—at our side we didn't feel as though we were amongst our own. The more of the ritual we shared the more we had the sensation that we were foreign to his faith. Finally, we left the apartment and took two buses. Malika went on one and I went on another. We headed toward the same destination, which is why I was surprised not to notice the absurdity of us each traveling on our own.

The scene greatly resembles that which I visualized the night before Cherifa was run over. The bus where I saw her in the company of her son's wife—Rajmana—was similar. The difference between the trip I undertook after leaving the Sunni's house and the previous one is that I now find myself alone. Malika is making a similar journey but on another bus. When I least expect it we arrive at my destination: an esplanade. The bus Malika traveled on is no longer present. It arrived a few moments ago and just departed. Curiously, instead of asking the driver to follow it, I get off to run and catch up to it. Perhaps I trust too much in my speed. I remember the day that I followed the green car that the sheikha and Nadira, the dervish who was furious with me because of the matter of the sheikha's appearance in *Playboy* magazine, traveled in for a few meters. I think that Malika's bus will hopelessly disappear. What's more, I don't understand the reason why my backpack, with all of my belongings in it, especially my computer with everything I have written in my life up to that moment, travels on that vehicle. Perhaps Malika did me the favor of carrying it when we left the apartment where we made our prayers. The esplanade is located in the middle of the desert. I run a few meters. I despair because I can't tell Malika that we should form a new mosque, one for emergencies, for when the rest of the practitioners aren't present. I am convinced that two parallel mosques are needed. Someone says that that would be bad. I don't know who affirms it so. Perhaps it is just a voice of the desert, which I hear while I run. But remembering, I know that that phrase is said by one of the characters portrayed in my last book. The husband of the woman of high lineage pronounces it. He has said those words without moving a millimeter from the bed where he is lying. The book remains in its place. Not a page has moved.

The character portrayed in the book adds that a second mosque would just cause greater confusion. Already this year they have had enough with the appearance of a mystic dream published in *Playboy* magazine, with a dervish's getting run over on the same corner as the house of prayer, and with the sheikha's visit to a hospital's emergency room. "God frees us from repeating these happenings twice," he pronounces. I realize then that I do not know what this man is sick with. His wife never clarified it for me. It could be that his state of health has deteriorated for some motive of a spiritual order. It could also be that he has been sickened by the constant company of the dogs.

The sheikha adds, I don't know if to the man with the book on his chest or to me myself as passenger in her ramshackle Datsun, that she had arranged the appointment with the plumber that same day, a little before feeling bad. She did it convinced that the mosque could no longer endure flaws of such magnitude. As much as she had begged a certain Hazim—who gives everything—my sick friend, the situation was intolerable. The mosque was at the point of turning into one of the few that would deny the faithful the right to ablution. And worse still to the pilgrims, an important cornerstone of the order. To give asylum to those who found themselves on pilgrimage is one of the first obligations that any dervish must observe. Precisely Hazim himself, I believe, was a pilgrim that arrived to the mosque during a night of prayer. I know so because the sheikha on that occasion paid great attention to his person. I have always noticed that particularity in the sheikha's conduct. Many times she prefers to talk only to new people. "While you are called Hazim nothing bad will be able to happen to you," she said as soon as she discovered him. Nonetheless, the sheikha does not know that he is my sick companion, with whom it has been my duty to circle around certain unknown mosques, which appear every once in a while as if from nowhere, on more than one occasion. "The palace is the same palace, no matter how far it is, no matter how ancient it looks, it is the same palace and it is ready to receive us," he repeated each time that one of those mosques appeared in all its splendor before our eyes.

One time, behind the sheikha's back, Hazim began to speak aloud. He said that the palaces could be used freely, that they could be entered freely, that ablutions could be performed however one wished. In that manner the pilgrims would see fresh water flow in a spontaneous manner. He affirmed likewise that the inhabitants of the surrounding area would only hear the divine call in this way. Knowing that a crystalline water awaited them. I thought of the apartment buildings that surrounded the mosque. I imagined the families that inhabited them. I saw them leaving their everyday tasks soon to go outside to encounter that strange voice. "And their hearts will become jubilant at hearing it," Hazim typically ended the discourses he pronounced when the sheikha was not present. I never learned why he preached during the sheikha's absences. I imagine that to her Hazim's words could seem even pleasing. Hazim, as is known, was a sick pilgrim. And the words pronounced by someone like that would inevitably be agreeable to the sheikha. She had always said that pilgrimage and the quality of martyrdom are the common element shared by the order's saints. I was in agreement with a similar idea. I know that all the saints are pilgrims. I know that all are sick. I also know that there does not exist any one saint in particular. They are all the same saint. It is this theme that I discuss in my last published book. In the book where two characters, despite appearing in bad light, are pleased with the work. Nonetheless, I have a set of obsessions that impede my being clear. The Izcuintepozoli dogs, for example, the article appearing in *Playboy* magazine, Nuh's death, the lack of attention I received at the hospital. Cherifa's being run over. The Muslim woman removing bills from her cleavage. The voice I imitated as a child pretending to be a servant seeking work. The traveling cobblers trying to make from my arm a decent gadget. The tragic death of my friend in a town near the border. The dog that managed to return from the zoo to its house by means of smell alone. Nonetheless, until the sheikha gets out of her Datsun there is little that can be talked about.

The sheikha tells me that there's not a single person that has not told her to get rid of her car. I remember on more than one occasion that a stone had to be made use of to strike the car's battery and in this way manage to start it. She would know perfectly the appropriate moment to give up the car. She confirms that she is tired of those who always want to indicate to her the correct conduct for a sheikha to observe. She will get out of the Datsun by her own means. Nonetheless, once she gets out she kneels. She holds her stomach with both hands and confirms that now she has been cured of everything. With a decisive step she heads toward the house. I can note that the tassels of her shoes drag across the muddy lot. I remain confused. Meanwhile, in the backseat, the servant continues not to say a word.

A Character in Modern Appearance

At the time, I don't remember the reasons why this happened, I had a German girlfriend. The girl actually belonged to a community of a kind of ethnic Germans, who for unclear reasons had lived for many generations on the Austro-Italian border. Her father ran a ski club in the Alps. He invited me more than once. However, for some reason that does not now come to mind, an invitation of that nature seemed like complete nonsense. She was beautiful and of modern appearance. She was interested in letters, had an affinity for literature, although I do not know what it was she studied. At that time I was looking for a car. Obviously not a normal car. I insisted on getting a Renault 5 from the seventies. One in good condition. I could not believe that such a perfect design would go unnoticed by so much of the population. I made many calls to the ads that appeared in the newspaper classifieds. I got to know, chasing the trail of these cars, some of the city's outskirts. By now, it was the second half of the '90s, the market had almost discarded those cars. They had been confined to the suburbs. It was very rare to see them on the main avenues, unless they were driven by a lover of those cars, as I thought that I would shortly become.

Although, as things have occurred, it is impossible that at that time I could have had a German girlfriend. Especially considering that my father is a simple agricultural technician—in fact a surveyor, my mother is a housewife, and I am the youngest daughter of the family. Since childhood I have been told I look like a little doll. Perhaps they refer to one of those figures that the residents of the community we live in are so fond of. Those that sometimes appear in puppet theaters. I have two brothers. One works for an airline, which only flies domestic flights. The other is a builder and the father of three children. It's strange that at my age—I'm forty-six—and with my figure—as I pointed out, I look like a doll—I can be considered someone's aunt. Less still a German woman's girlfriend. But in this case I am the aunt of the three children of my brother the builder. A loving aunt, too. When I can, I steal something from my father's wallet and buy them some candies. Despite acting freely, I feel very strange when I get to the shop around the corner from my house. I always worry that the clerk will notice that it is stolen money. But I know that I'm saved by the age that I appear to be, not by that I really am.

But, despite my circumstances, I insist that at the time I had a German girlfriend. With whom, furthermore, I went to buy a Renault 5. In a way that is not unusual for me, to get that car I contacted, through one of the newspapers that offer secondhand goods, a series of strange individuals. I knew, for example, someone who, besides selling his own car, which for some mysterious reason he did not recommend, knew of one in perfect condition, which its owners didn't want to sell either, and whose owner lived about 20 miles away. The man promised to talk to that person to convince him to get rid of his vehicle. I found it all so unusual, I immediately gave him my phone number. Interestingly he called me two days later to say he had spoken to the owner but had not yet managed to change his mind. He needed reinforcements, he said. We should go together to speak with him personally. He ended the conversation by describing the car. Red with a cream interior. When he finished he gave me the details to meet the following evening. At the gate of a cemetery located in the suburbs, the last stop on a suburban metro line, he said. He would drive me in his own car, which he said it gave him some embarrassment to show me, to the man's house.

To me all these instructions struck me as normal. Although I'm sure that most anyone would have given up at having to go to meet a stranger at the gate of a cemetery. But I grew up moving between an infinity of the city's zones—I know them all equally, and cannot consider any of them foundational to my development. I abhor them all. We were thrown out of every house amidst threats. I do not know if my father did not pay rent on time or if deadlines specified in the contracts were met too quickly. The fact is that more than once I had to dance folk dances in front of their owners, hoping they would thereby take mercy on our situation. Since I turned thirty years old I have been doing that regularly. That is, since even before I mastered Castilian. I remember that the landlord used to sit on one of the main cushions, furious, and I began to move my body like a real puppet. Step, step, step, I took a few steps to the left. Step, step, step, a few more to the right. On the ceiling of the room my father had installed an ingenious system, composed of very thin nylon strings, which gave the impression that my steps were led by someone very talented at that art. However, none of the owners I danced for ever changed their mind. They waited for me to finish the entire show, some lasting four hours or more, the longest those that attempted to display my feelings towards Mother Nature. But eventually they gave the order to their men to begin the eviction. In a few minutes, all our things would be on the street. My mother was made to mourn, despite her military honors. She knelt in the center of the room and, yelling, she regretted joining a descendant of slave dealers—my father's ancestors had made their living transporting them from Africa to America—in concubinage. Meanwhile, I had to untangle the cords that had made me a puppet for a few hours, not knowing where to take refuge. Other family members would then appear, one by one. Some already carrying their belongings: the airline employee, the builder, his wife and three children. They all surrounded our father, who, disoriented, did not know what attitude to assume. He should take responsibility for his family. Especially for me, since I am the youngest of the siblings. My little nephews, for whom I habitually had to become a sort of thief, could not compete with me and take away the privilege of being the one most in need of care and protection.

I do not know what my German girlfriend would have thought of me, at that time, or of the people of this country. The case is that she accepted, quite naturally, my proposal to accompany me on my expedition in search of a Renault. We left at noon. It was summer. She wore a short skirt and a sleeveless top. Arriving at the subway station we encountered our first inconvenience. In those days they had annoyingly changed the fares. The ticket no longer cost the same whole denomination; they had added a ridiculous fraction to it, but enough so that long lines were formed at the ticket counters. Everyone, both cashiers and users, were overwhelmed by the change. It occurred to me to avoid this huge number of people by using the small door for disabled access, which is always beside the automatic controllers. We had to put on a small act, because there were two of us trying to get through. I hunched as far over as I could, faking paralysis. My girlfriend had to play the role of the nurse. I had to hold on to her like my stability depended on her presence. We went through that way. In front of a policeman so surprised he had no choice but to let us pass. I do not understand why, but at that moment, standing on the other side, was a journalist from the cultural section of a major newspaper. What was he doing there? Was he expecting someone? In this case it was useless to try to explain the relationship between the change in the price of the tickets and my hunched figure, assisted by a beautiful woman, in the proscribed area of the subway.

My reputation was at stake before this reporter. It was likely he would publish a notice in the newspaper where he worked, saying he had seen me try to travel for free without my puppet costume on. I wanted to tell him that I felt like a rabbit just before dying. But I didn't. Perhaps that seemed to me to be a similar figure because my favorite childhood activity was raising animals. I even kept small zoos in some of the houses we lived in, dismantling them as soon as we received the eviction notices. Until, in an instant, I decided not to continue pursuing that activity. That happened when I was about to turn forty, and my father ordered me to dedicate myself to a job commensurate with my sex and my situation. I think he was considering the possibility of my forming my own family. It was an option that terrified me. I was not prepared for it. My father would certainly choose someone from among his friends. I didn't even want to think about it. I would have preferred to continue the activity of standing at supermarket doors offering animals for sale. They say that I looked very funny, with my slender figure next to my bicycle, which had a small cage installed behind it. At that time I was no less than thirty-five years old. It was sheer madness to spend hours out alone on the street, offering passersby the offspring of my cats, my doves, my squirrels. Sometimes I also wore my lab rats. I had them well trained so that they would sit on my shoulder, thus keeping away the men who would overstep the bounds of propriety. Too bad the fiercest of them, which repelled them in an efficient manner, died at the hands of my brother, the airline employee. I do not know what repulsion it caused in him. What feelings my delicate animal aroused in him. Anyway, one morning, while all slept in the great room that my father had made suitable, my brother got up before the customary time and went to my tiny zoo, from which he removed my favorite rat. Before that he had put a pot of water on to boil in the kitchen, and he threw the animal in it without any kind of compassion. That is why, in order to avoid provoking in my brother incomprehensible feelings again, I almost never leave the house with any of the rats that I own. In the cage I installed on the bike, every animal has its compartment. I do not want species to eat each other, or for them to breed inconvenient crosses. Apart from being alone on the street, another problem I face during my stays in front of supermarkets is the subject of charging for sales. I'm not used to handling money. In my house they have always banned me from it. My father has considered money sinful. His relationship with it has always been heavily regulated. He has never had it, but he defends the coins that he's been able to treasure. He allows himself to make small deals, like the one established with my animals, as well as other smaller transactions. That allows him to at times procure small amounts. Although I have knowledge that he once claimed a not-so-modest sum, when he worked as a surveyor for the state to build a highway that would link the north to the south of our city.

After that trip on the subway, which I managed without further mishap with my German girlfriend occupying the seat reserved for the disabled, we had to wait about half an hour in front of the appointed cemetery. The figure of a gigantic man suddenly appeared, with a large overbite and rather small eyes, and told us, with stammering words, that he never would have imagined that I would have kept my promise to show up there. But it seems that his biggest surprise was to see who had accompanied me to the meeting. He looked fascinated by the presence of my German girlfriend. He said he now felt more shame than ever to show us his Renault 5, although he said that it was red like the one we were going to visit. Finally, after a series of questions, he agreed to let us climb into his car. He had parked a little ways out because he first wanted to make sure, if we appeared, what kind of person I was. When we saw his car we noticed that it was wrecked. It only had part of its body. Nonetheless, he noted that the engine was in excellent condition. That it made a little noise but that was normal. He didn't want to invest money in mufflers that could well be used to make a number of improvements to increase its power. We climbed in. The seats seemed to have been scratched by a herd of wild cats. The smell of oil, of a machine shop, was more than pervasive. We started the trip. Indeed, the small car was fast. Unstable too. We moved at the highest possible speed and felt how it jostled from one side of the road to the other. We could barely hear what the man told us. The speed and strong engine noise made any communication impossible. We could understand that he was showing us a number of places. In general, the jail and some other cemeteries. It was strange how he slowed down when we passed the zone's main hospital. He showed it to us in great detail. Some kilometers later he took a side street.

I was not afraid. I'm more than used to dealing with strangers. I've become accustomed to them at the doors of supermarkets, where I usually do my pre-sales. People select their chosen animal, I place a mark on its ear, and later they must come to the house to make the relevant negotiations with my father. The last time, a few months ago, there was a real disaster. We had to leave the house we inhabited as soon as possible—the threat of eviction was already imminent—and my father did business with a Mr. Dufo to buy my little rabbit nursery. It was ten specimens of Flemish Giants. Mr. Dufo, an old acquaintance of my father, came with his fat kids in a small Karmanghia to dismantle everything. The cages were carried out in minutes. A week later we went to collect the first payment. We entered the patio of his house, and what impressed me most was that the rabbits began to despair in their cages as soon as they recognized me. It seems that Mr. Dufo did not feed them as one should. I wanted to tell my father, but his look silenced me. I was not surprised. I know that anyone could accuse me of whatever they wanted and that my father would always prove them right. At that time, for example, despite the grievance of not paying for the animals and, above all, of not having fed them, he laughed with his friend.

As I mentioned, I was not afraid. The man steering the ramshackle Renault turned onto a side street. From that moment things changed. A kind of sense of relief seemed to install itself inside the car, although it was not normal to feel something like that, for the words that the subject was incessantly uttering, and which we had heard haltingly, had led us into a kind of uneasiness. But the noise of the engine, at lowering its volume, at least allowed us to listen to each other, which seemed visibly to reassure us. Although that's not absolutely true because the presence of such a disagreeable man and his extreme interest in prisons, cemeteries, and hospitals made me uneasy. In appearance there was nothing to see in the landscape. Although there were two junkyards of cars. In an act I now consider childlike, I tried to find some Renault among the mountains of piled cars. My quick search was useless. The man then began to ask us personal questions. First he inquired about how my girlfriend and I had met. If we loved each other a lot. If we practiced what all couples supposedly practiced. I watched as that subject, from time to time, glanced at my girlfriend in the rearview mirror. I preferred to keep my view on the landscape.

The car kept going. I asked if we were close and, strangely, the man replied that we were never close to anything. But that yes, we had always been close to the car we sought. I asked questions about the specific characteristics of that car, like if it still had the original parts and things like that. I was alarmed when I noticed that the man did not follow the thread of the conversation. It was the first time since we initiated our first communication over the telephone that we were not immersed fully in the world of the Renault 5. He continued asking personal questions, which were increasingly daring. I noticed that something had changed. Though his physical appearance was almost the same: his giant, malformed body, his protruding teeth and small eyes. The only noticeable difference was his body's manner of sweating. Especially on the sides of his shirt.

I think I'm something of a liar. I repeat that it is not true that I had a German girlfriend and that I never, what's more, have thought about the possibility of buying a car. Even a Karmanghia like that which both my ballet teacher and the unpleasant Mr. Dufo own. Nor is it true that they threw us out of the houses where we lived by court order. We didn't always leave them by being scared away by their landlords. There was at least a chance that things were different. Instead of a court order, one morning we encountered immense vehicles waiting outside the door. They were going to demolish the house. It was our family home, where we had always lived. Our problems as tenants came later. Precisely because we were stripped of the house we inherited from my ancestors. Which we had maintained from the time our family's first navigator settled in the country. They were going to build a highway, which would link the north and south of the city, which crossed through the living room. My father seems to have intuited that situation many years before. It happened one morning when I was trying on some flesh-colored stockings to celebrate the completion of primary school. It was an important moment in my life. I was the only one in the room who could wear socks like that. I was going to leave my studies forever. My father got out of bed saying he had dreamed that he was a stray dog wandering around town. Arriving at the supposed family home, he found a highway in its place. With vehicles traveling at high speed in one direction and the other. He woke up when a car nearly hit him. I tried not to listen to his story and kept trying on my stockings. It seemed somewhat funny to me to imagine my father becoming a stray dog. I asked myself how a dog would survive without money. I told him. I warned him that he could not have turned into a stray dog.

The Renault man suggested stopping to drink a few beers. He spoke of a place, not far from the road, where he was very well known. Unexpectedly, without giving us time to answer, he changed course. When we arrived we noticed that three Renault 5s were parked by the cantina's door. I thought one of them was the one we had come for. The subject dashed my erroneous assumption, saying the man determined to keep his car never left his house. Indeed, this was the reason that the car was in such good condition, but that absurd immobility was something that could not continue to be allowed. It was then that I remembered certain events prior to the encounter with that enormous man, at the cemetery gate where we arranged our meeting. The mass of people on the subway. Our transit through the free lane for the disabled. I also remembered my encounter with the cultural journalist. His face of astonishment when he saw me appear. My girlfriend hugging me, watching my steps as if I might fall at any moment. Opposite the cantina, seeing the three cars, I asked myself about the reasons for my interest in these cars in particular. The man kept talking. My girlfriend was trapped in the backseat. The car was stopped. The annoying afternoon sun fell through the windows. The heat was stifling. The engine stopped running. I wondered if the phone number of that man, which had appeared in the newspaper classifieds, was actually his. The man got out of the car. Without closing the door he went into the cantina. I looked back. I imagined what my German girlfriend's father, who lived in the Alps, would think then, seeing his daughter sitting on the rickety seat. Could it have really been a pack of cats that destroyed the upholstery? Within a few minutes I saw the gigantic man approaching. He was accompanied by two other subjects. Each wore a shirt with the

Renault logo on it. Perhaps, I thought, in front of the ski cabin, where the father was attending to holiday skiers, a Renault was also occasionally parked. We decided to leave that place. I started walking. Faster and faster. Just then, with four Renault 5s in front of a cantina in the background, I understood, despite having the scene behind me, the real reasons why I thought at the time that I had a German girlfriend, or rather, a girlfriend of German ancestry. Although, now I don't remember them well. What reasons could I have had to have a girlfriend? Nonetheless, I have no regrets at all about the experience. However, I do experience some guilt every time I remember that I told my father that he could not even reach-the category of dog. And all because of his relationship with money. I do not know if I said it out loud. In other words, I do not even know if I formulated it. I think that having wanted to insult my father was due to the state of nerves that leaving school, where I had studied for almost twenty years, put me in. It seems that the director had spoken to my father; she had arranged it behind my back, telling him that I was already a young lady and that there was little they could do for me. There was no way for me to even learn to write my name correctly. Instead of writing it with a *J*, as was the custom, I insisted on using a *Y*. So I wrote it on all the papers put before me. Especially on the exam sheets. I was already a young lady, the teachers told me so again and again, so, unlike the other students who wore their wool socks, I should use flesh-colored nylons. My mother seemed the most excited about the idea. She begged my father for permission on more than one occasion. My father had the final decision. If he allowed it he would have to go by himself to the warehouses downtown to ask for them. He would seek, obviously, the cheapest ones. Now it was easy to find them in all price ranges. They imported them from many parts of the world. It was not the same during the time of war, my mother told me. Perhaps that accounts for her enthusiasm. She told me that she did not dare to tell me what she and her friends had been willing to do to acquire them when the freedom fighters took our city.

She was nervous, as can be imagined. I was finally finishing my primary education. At that time I could have no idea what the future would hold for me. At school I had been a terrible student. Especially in science and math. Not to mention the problems I had with quantum physics and trigonometry, subjects which were curiously not in the curriculum but which my father insisted that I memorize. The schools where I was enrolled were of an absolute misery. I suffered from teachers' threats at all times. They said that in my circumstances I was unable to follow a normal academic life. The only one that seemed to feel some affection for me was the ballet teacher, the owner of a green Karmanghia with a white roof, just like Mr. Dufo. But perhaps this is not entirely true. With our minimal resources it is unlikely that my school had dance lessons. All the dances. The step, step, step, left and step, step, step, right that I have invented. According to the teachers a black future awaited me. So, sometimes, I decided to escape from school with a little friend, with whom I shared my fondness for animals, we went to visit people who had placed newspaper advertisements informing that they were selling pets. One time we had an unpleasant experience with an old man who offered hamsters for sale, who shut himself in a bathroom with my girlfriend for an indefinite period. I only heard her through the door, crying. I started to do the puppets number. I think I even invented some capers. It started out better than ever. It occurred to me to do a short number for this occasion. No more than five minutes. There was no one to see me do it. Unfortunately the door was closed. When he finally opened it and I could see my friend again, I was no longer a puppet but was instead reduced to being someone who wrote *Y* instead of *J* on her exam sheets, confusing the first letter of my name. This old man gave us a couple of small animals before we left. I remember one was white and one was pink. As much as I tried to encourage my friend on the way back, I could not. I also tried unsuccessfully to do a musical number using small hamsters. I bound their front legs and forced them to dance. In the end, her sadness was so great that we decided to let the little pets loose and say goodbye without even a kiss. Then I had to find another friend; for me it was very easy to make them. With her I ventured to the veterinary school, which was on the outskirts of the city, where we stole a newborn pig. My family, to my amazement, adopted him as a pet. Since then I could not free myself from the anxiety caused by hearing my father tell us—my mother, my brothers, and nephews, all of us gathered in the big bed—the sad fate suffered by pigs during the war. My grandparents had had one in their house at the time. They always kept it tied to the tub. Since there were electricity problems, and since that amount of dead flesh could not have been preserved in good condition for very long, they would eat it bit by bit. They cut off the piece destined for their food each day, and diligently treated its wounds right away. After half a year, the pig was just a living trunk. My father recalled that the animal died for no apparent reason. All of a sudden, one morning they found it inert in the bathtub. It even died on a day when they had not planned to slice off any cut of meat.

When I had almost no notion of the future life I would lead, when I could not even remotely imagine that a gigantic man would take my girlfriend and me on a rural road, our family home was demolished. As is known, a freeway that would unite the north and south of the city would pass through the living room. I remember looking, with my father, at the remains of the demolition. Surely he wanted, at that time, to sell anything that had remained undamaged. Some doors and windows that the usurers who often post up around the demolitions buy. The previous days he had already sold a large number of pieces, but there could still be something of hidden value. I could see nothing but rubble. Interestingly, amidst the disaster, no traces appeared of the fleas that had plagued me while I lived in that house. My mother told me. She said that sometimes, totally hopeless from itching, I escaped naked into the street. I removed my clothes, skirts, petticoats, and high heels to go out to a dust cloud that stretched in front of the main facade. As my mother told me, the greatest shame my body exhibited was my skin riddled with pitting. My mother made a ball, formed of several socks, which she placed under the sheets of the big bed, which the whole family shared, except for our grandparents, who had a pair of bunks located to each side. Fleas, once satiated by our blood, sought refuge in that ball for the heat that the socks' texture offered. The next day it was very easy to take that ball full of fleas, throw it in a pot of boiling water, dry it out, and put it back under the sheets.

Once the demolition was carried out, my grandparents were turned over to some charitable souls. We never saw them again. They were adopted, so to speak, by people who lived across the railroad tracks. That line was what had always marked our stock. It was one thing to live on this side, and quite another to have your house across the tracks. Although my grandmother said that she had the opportunity to buy a very nice lot in the main area. The downside is that it had an oblong shape. Maybe that's why, after the demolition, my father, to give my grandparents, in their last moments, some satisfaction, turned them over to some people on the other side. My father hung a sign on each of them that mentioned that they needed to be picked up by some kind soul. My father knew, he told me once when I rebelled and did not want to continue playing the role of the small doll, that the charitable souls to which he referred had the mission of transporting the lost elderly to the ends of the city. When I found that out, I became very worried about what would have happened during that trance with my grandmother's spaniel, because, as will be seen later, she left the demolition carrying her little dog in her arms. I remember having seen them, first my grandfather and then my grandmother, a day later, crossing the railway tracks. I remember it well because I had that famous book of trigonometry under my arm, the surveyor's bible, according to my father. The next day I had to take a test, which unfortunately never took place. My father told me it was a shame that his youngest daughter would reject all mathematical subjects, so spoiled and pampered.

It seems absurd for me to refer with such interest to mathematical sciences. Especially now, when I remember the anxiety that my grandmother must have sensed when the notice arrived that the house would be demolished. It was, as we know, located right in the middle of the path of the highway that would link the north and south of the city. Nobody knows it, but my father was one of the men who made up the crew of surveyors who had to map the motorway's route. Duty first, he said on more than one occasion. It wouldn't have cost him anything to make his measurements a little crooked, thereby affecting more houses on the other side. But those houses belonged to families that did have the right to a full life. So he made the most direct line between north and south, resulting in our living room's being compromised. Perhaps he also did so, somehow, so that his dream of turning into a skeletal stray dog, with no trace of money, that searched for its family home through an inferno of cars, might come true. My grandmother did not leave the house until the time of the demolition. My grandfather had been turned over to charitable souls the day before. We also stayed inside until the machines arrived, but we settled in the back shed, which at the time we thought would be spared from the push of the machines. They removed my grandmother almost by force. The rest of the family's complaints were worthless. Leaving a house about to be demolished, my grandmother looked like an old lady who had been stripped of her fortune. And she was. She was accompanied, as is known, by her spaniel. The dog was a rare breed then. I had acquired it once when I visited a family of foreigners who put out an ad in the newspapers. I remember that on that occasion I was driving my car alone. I left as if nothing—it still was not even close to the time to leave—through the front door of the school where I studied. I got in the car, which I used to leave parked near one of the corners, and set off, paying special attention to the address that appeared in the newspaper. The spaniel was so rare at the time that it was the symbol of the country's canine association.

That's not true, I never owned any car. Not the Renault 5 I once tried to visit in the areas surrounding the city, nor a green Karmanghia with a white roof, similar to the one that belonged to my hypothetical ballet teacher and to the man who got my rabbits without paying a penny in return. I never bought my grandmother a dog. Although it was true that there was a spaniel, which they named after a brand of girls panties that were very popular at that time. We could not have known that the machines would sweep everything away. We were not given time to prepare. So my brother's belongings were lost, his aeronautical uniform, which he wore once a month when he had to receive his superiors, the big bed, which the entire family slept in, my little nephews' bottles, my gigantic makeup bag, which I sometimes used to paint myself to look younger than I really am, the cages for rats, hamsters, and rabbits, the pair of Siamese cats, the pots and stove. And, worst of all, they lightly wounded my mother, who, I think, shared some of the blame for having wanted to hold on until the end to the silk stockings and imported cigarettes, which, with great effort, she had managed to get the revolutionary forces to give to her. They were not the same stockings I wore when I graduated from elementary school; those were nylon, and were cheaper than cheap, at least that's what my father said, who was the only one qualified to make, himself, in person, the family's purchases. That was a horror. We felt then for the first time the feeling of literally being on the street with all our belongings uncovered. Some of the animals escaped. Apparently, if we take for granted what I'm telling, at that time, when we lived in the house behind the family home, I was already raising my animals. But I'm sure I did not yet have my little zoo in order. My pets were loose. They climbed into and out of the big bed all the time. There were many. I remember from that time a couple of rats, three rabbits, two cats, a very old dog, which almost couldn't move, and the pig that, little by little, had begun to grow. For me, the strengthening of the animal meant an increasing torture. Eventually the animal was donated by my father to a gambling den that he had a relationship with, to be eaten by the players. When I first brought it to our family home we had to feed it with a bottle, which it used alternatingly with one of my nephews. My brother the builder told me that he would lend me his child's bottle if I also took care of feeding the child. That's why I spent all my time bottle-feeding them both. Five minutes for the pig. Five minutes for my nephew. Until the milk was gone. But the pig grew much faster than the creature. And it developed the tenderest feelings toward us. It became the ideal pet. It followed me everywhere, even when I stole some money from my father's wallet and went to the store to buy candy. The pig was more faithful to me than to anyone else. Even more than the rat that years later, when I was forty-two, I began to carry on my shoulder. But I could not bring it to class. In contrast to the rat. Since animals were banned at the school, I left it at a nearby sewer. It leaped in and disappeared into the vents; hours later, when I returned, one whistle was enough for it to climb back out onto my shoulder. The problem with the pig was that as it fattened up and proved to be a better pet than the others, my father began to threaten that he would eat it on the least expected day. A pig is an animal that is only raised to be eaten, he declared with his natural logic. Thus he demonstrated his certainty in predestination and fate. Just as he had been chosen to be poor and despised all his life, the only reason for pigs to exist was to be eaten by man. I was kicking, screaming, pulling out my hair. On more than one occasion I even threatened my father that I would never put my folk dress back on again. I was not going to allow my pig to be killed or for it to occur to him to subject it to a regime like the one that never left the bathtub.

One of the main characteristics of my personality is lying all the time. I think that this, somehow, makes me amusing to others. I know that the stories that the puppets interpret always have a lie at their center. Maybe that's why I have assimilated aspects of my performances into my daily life. I lie, for example, about my age. I love to say I am forty-six when in fact I am just forty-five years old. I always lie to the store's salesman, as many know that I tend to buy sweets for my nephews with money stolen from my father's wallet. I lie about my hobbies. It is not true that I had a trigonometry book under my arm when my grandfather crossed the railroad tracks. That is false. I am actually interested in writing books. Making them, inventing them, writing them. I know that I can hardly write my name. Instead of a *J* I always put a *Y*. Nonetheless, almost no one knows it, but I made a book about dogs. So that my father leaves me alone I've covered it with a famous trigonometry book's dust jacket. It is divided into three parts. The first is a description of all the breeds I know. Absolutely every one I have ever seen in my life. On the way from my house to school and from my school to the house. It is actually the only route I have ever traveled. And when, after its demolition, we had to leave our family home and started moving from one lease to another, the decision was made that I would study no further. It's a lie, therefore, that I escaped with a little friend to answer newspaper ads for pet sales. It is not true that once my friend was locked inside with an old man who raised hamsters while I danced like a puppet in front of the bathroom door. Of course the spaniel breed has been given a privileged place in the book that I have written in hiding from others. In some newspapers once I found a selection of drawings of different dogs. I carefully cut them out and pasted each one next to the descriptions I make of them. The second part is devoted to working animals. There is the firefighter's Dalmatian, the policeman's shepherds, and the Saint Bernards saving people in the snow. The third is dedicated to dog heroes. In that one I have invented a set of stories about animals saving their masters, and the punishments that many receive when they display poor conduct. One time a lady, whose dog ripped up a very old plant, tied the animal up with its own leash, so that the dog could not lie down. He had to remain seated all the time. He had to stay in one position all night. It had to be another dog belonging to the same lady, one which did display impeccable conduct, that used its teeth to break the leash used to carry out the punishment. In my family everyone laughed when I spoke of the existence of such a book. Especially my father, who was burdened by my resounding failure in primary school. But I lie, I say things that are not true at every opportunity. For example, I repeat, I have never had a car. I'm not even fit to drive. I never succeeded when I wanted to sporadically escape from elementary school. With all the makeup I wear—with the heels, the miniskirts that I occasionally wear since my father told me that at my age I am fit to make a family of my own and that I should sweet-talk some man—it is impossible for the school gatekeeper not to notice that I intend to escape. How could I get—especially considering that instead of putting *J* I write a *Y* to begin my name—a driver's license. Impossible. Nobody seems to understand that I'm just a family's spoiled daughter, whose greatest virtue is dance, especially the dance of the puppets. Actually, the spaniel my grandmother took was a vulgar cocker mutt, which I saw her trade, some cloudy morning, with a poor woman who in exchange gave her several branches of roses she grew in her garden.

My father, seeing that the bulldozers must continue with their work, immediately put the sign on my grandmother's chest and made her cross the railroad tracks. Grandmother never let the dog fall from her arms. Immediately afterwards he disappeared in the streets on this side of town. He was probably going to find a place that would give us shelter. He would be desperately looking for a place to rent. It would be the first of our existence. The series of tortures that the whole family would suffer over the following years, when the landlords would mercilessly take our things out to the street, again and again, would begin then. Even now that I am actually forty-five years old I cannot help but feel the terrible fear of an imminent eviction. When I feel one of these about to happen, I will immediately look for my folk dancing costume. I mentally review the step, step, step, right. The step, step, step, left. I remember that in the midst of the demolition of the family home, I sought to be protected by my three nephews, who seemed to be the only ones who understood my state of nerves. My two brothers, both the builder and the airline employee, sat beside their suitcases. They remained impassive, waiting for my father to resolve the situation. My mother, slightly hurt, held the objects obtained after the liberation forces entered the city. The animals were sniffing around. To see the scene of everyone together without a roof to shelter us made me realize that my brother's children, my little nephews, for whom I stole a coin from my father on more than one occasion, did not have a mother in order. I realized at that moment that they had never had one. Nor, apparently, had they ever needed one. They had appeared in the family suddenly. I was so scared I did not worry about any of my belongings. Except my trigonometry textbook, which the book of dogs that I had written was underneath. My animals, at that time, had the opportunity to do whatever they pleased. About an hour later my father returned, bringing with him my first folk costume. It was very colorful. It was the one that I began to use from that point on. The presence of this costume took me out of my self-absorption. I had not realized the bustle that had begun to develop beyond my immediate family. I had had eyes only for the removal of my grandmother. I was still watching her, though surely the group of charitable souls on the other side had already found her. I had not noticed the men in the demolition machines, which had given an immediate, brief deadline to remove our things from the center of events. As I said, the family home was completely destroyed, but not the shack where we were, which had only been partially damaged thanks to a fortuitous breakdown of the machinery. A cloud of dust rose before us. Apart from the demolition workers, separated by a security tape, a crowd of people was present. Then, very gently, my father began to undress me. He started by removing my long skirt, my pleated bodice, and my petticoat. At one point I was totally naked. I sensed that my father was doing so with the secret intention that someone, from among the multitudes, would want to become my husband and, thus, surely take a weight off his shoulders. I do not know what I was thinking, something completely absurd, no doubt. I could not imagine that my father wanted to get rid of me at the time. It was ridiculous. My father would be incapable of having such a thought—I was the youngest in the family, the spoiled little girl. Not even my dear nephews had been able to displace me. Once I was naked he began to very gently put on the dress he had brought me. I do not know how but he had also prepared small strips of transparent nylon, the same I later used for my presentations for the landlords. He tied them to my wrists and ankles. Then he climbed over to what remained of the wall. Though I had never before been in a similar circumstance, I knew perfectly what was expected of me. I became, from that moment, a real doll. Everyone else, the workers, the curious located behind the security tape, and my family, watched my father's movements in silence. From the delicate undressing to my transformation into a puppet. I was eager to move. I rehearsed the prancing to be undertaken in my mind. Step, step, step... several steps to the right. Step, step, step, to the left now. But no, I should not wait until the appearance of certain men, landlords called by my father, whom my graceful figure, that of a girl just out of primary school, should convince. I would persuade them to obtain a covered space for my animals, my father and my mother, my two brothers, my three adorable nephews, and me. That day, the first I did it on, my dance was a success that was never repeated. My brothers helped my father to climb onto the remains of the wall. From there he managed the strings attached to my wrists and my ankles. But when they arrived, the landlords showed no reaction. Instead the crowd, including those responsible for the demolition, applauded furiously. Despite the enthusiasm, the shed encountered the same fate as the family home. Sometimes I think about why I could never dance so well again. It must be because, since then and for quite some time—I think when I started to occupy myself with writing books—I thought too intensely about the art of puppetry. That was my downfall. Without realizing it I suddenly lost my freshness.

It is perhaps for this reason that my speech is a hybrid. Sometimes, to wind up confusing things, I stutter uncontrollably. I then go in search of a spoon to overcome these trances. I take the spoon—it can also be a fork or chopstick—and put it in front of me and I make it slowly spin. The stuttering ends when the ladle stops spinning. Although what happens next is almost always worse, because the lack of stuttering highlights the hybridity of my accents. So far, as I said, I have not fully mastered Castilian. But worst of all is that before this awkward learning there was no mother tongue for me. I am unable to communicate, just like that. I could barely learn the rest of the word that goes behind the *J* or *Y* of my name. Nonetheless, since I turned forty years old I have written books. First it was one about dogs, then another that made reference to a bigot, named Bernardo Cafloque, who by uselessly waiting on his boss, who sent him to buy gasoline on a trip that took three consecutive days, left a paralytic mother to rot in his house. Then the story of a woman, Rita Rojas, appeared, who at a popular party meets a man who later accompanies her to her house with the sole intention of stealing her television. Later I had as my character a person—I don't remember their name—who confuses the profession of an everyday woman with that of a saint. Finally I composed a story narrated by a family of rats. All this activity, of putting into writing a series of situations in a language that I went along inventing for the occasion, seemed to be obstructed by my obligations at primary school. I remember that the last year was the most difficult. As much as I yearned for it, I could only manage to memorize the two times table. And the panic that being a surveyor's daughter produced in me, since I should know the tangent is not the same as the cotangent, obligated me to convince my little friend, the one with whom I adventured to the veterinary school to steal the pig, to go to the markets, most of all at the end of the year, with the intention of stealing a number of bottles of liquor and giving them as gifts to the teachers to pass their courses. Every day I look fatter. It is strange that I perceive it. Fat, huge. It is very strange that this is my new constitution, if in reality I am no more than a graceful, popular puppet. It's as if there are two persons in me. That's without counting the facet of my personality that had a German girl as her girlfriend, with whom I chased after a Renault automobile. That thing of having several personalities, which can sound very obvious, in my case has a set of particularities that I am not sure if I want to share with anyone else. I know that I am a funny figure, that I seek to bring joy with my dances for the landlords, but I also know that I am no more than a fatty, who could calmly compete in fatness with the pig I stole some time ago. The same animal that my father killed with a sharp knife and whose cries I still hear. He did not heal the animal after the first attack, as was the custom during the war. He let it squeal and bleed out. He simply allowed things to happen. As he has always allowed them to happen. My father happy, pretending not to really notice what happens around him. Without taking sides with anyone or anything. Except for his lack of money. That's true, he would not allow, for any motive, for anyone to perturb the tranquility that that condition proportions to him. That is surely why he didn't charge Mr. Dufo a cent for my rabbits. Perhaps he thought that receiving such a payment would remove him from his condition. Although considering it well, perhaps it had to do with another matter, because then the money he accepted for drawing up the plans that resulted in the destruction of our family home would not make sense. Despite those contradictory, or perhaps camouflaged, behaviors, he would not have been in agreement if someone were to do something to remove him from his misery. But remove him how? It is not a matter of money. I don't think that it is. If someone were to deliver him large quantities he would charge himself with making them disappear, without their presence managing to modify his habitual behavior. That is why he killed the pig, whole, not in pieces, and sold it to the administrators of the gambling den. The killing was difficult. When he was halfway done, with the pig wounded and bleeding from its neck, he had to request help from the market's butcher, who finished the operation in a flash. But now the fat one is me. I do not know if it is true, in every case it is my brothers who tell me that I look this way. Could it be true? In that case I could no longer wear the folkloric dress that I do my performances with. I could no longer continue being the doll that everyone—except the landlords—admires. My father could not tie the nylon strings to my wrists and my ankles, which he uses to take me from one side of the room to the other.

I do not understand why we suffer so much with the matter of the houses. Taking into account that my brother says he is a builder. At least that is what I said when I introduced him. That one brother was a builder and the other the employee of a nonexistent aviation company that only offered domestic flights. Nonetheless, the builder brother has always been under the domain of my father, and my father is a person that has never allowed for anyone in his family to build anything. That would remove us, immediately, from the category of grieving family. That's why I believe that my father was who was in charge of baptizing the family members with some occupation that improvisationally occurred to him. With that being true, I don't know where we acquired the money for our subsistence. I don't think from my pre-sales of animals at the doors of grocery stores. I remember that very few were those that reached the door of the house after having shown interest in some pet. I especially remember a family of foreigners that wanted to acquire some Siamese kittens. First they bought one, and then the other. At the beginning they took a male, and then they asked me over the telephone to take them a female. When I arrived at the house, I noticed that the girl in the family had painted the first cat's foot an intense black. She seemed to have used a watercolor. I blushed at noticing it. I imagined an entire fantasy world. With her bedroom full of colored pencils, chalkboards, stuffed animals, and my cat in the midst of all that splendor. I thought about the look I displayed then. I was not a small figure or a monstrous fatty. I was an adolescent very similar to the foreign singers that appear on television. That's right, I used eyeglasses, with monstrous frames. I would have wanted to wear my hair longer, but my father had prohibited me from it. I have the image of the girl carrying the cat with the painted foot. I don't remember more, just that I said that I could not leave the second animal, because first they should pay my father. I remember that they performed the discourtesy of offering me the money. It seemed like a resounding lack of education. Then I must not have been more than thirty-six years old. How was it possible that those foreigners tried to humiliate me in such a way? I paused a few moments without saying a word. After a few minutes, I repeated that I had taken the second cat only so that they could see it but that they had to return to my house if they wanted to buy it. They did so. A day later they arrived at the door of the house that we rented at that time driving an immense car. Only the father and mother were there. The daughter had surely stayed playing with the cat with the painted foot. It amazed me to see the interest that they displayed in my merchandise. I think that at that time I offered on the streets a treasure that was difficult to comprehend. At that time Siamese cats were not bred like most are today. They maintained their elongated face, tubular body, and immense ears. Their tails curled at the end as if they were marsupials. I imagine the girl's face of happiness with the second cat between her arms. Always, since that date, I have had cats. I remember that on the roof of the destroyed house there was an apartment that my grandmother always maintained for rent. It was small and quite bright. On a certain occasion, between the departure of a tenant and the entrance of another, my father had to paint the walls. I accompanied him at his labor. At that time I was already an obedient girl. I was not, even remotely, the young woman with the square glasses or the disastrous woman that I later became. No sooner had we entered the apartment than we were attacked by a true army of fleas. It was curious to see them climbing inside and outside my clothes. Above my legs—on that occasion I had taken care to cover them with nylon stockings—and over my chest—my father had recently bought me a few bras called trainers. None of this matters to my father who, as is known, was a surveyor. I ask myself how I could represent such a father in film form. Especially now that there are plans to make a filmed autobiography of myself. An autobiography whose axis would be each of the books that I have published. Texts, although in appearance they don't take place anywhere or refer to any particular aspect of reality, that each have, at least in my head, a determined place and circumstance. Like, for example, the story of the visit, on the next day, to the remains of the family home. The most dazzling thing about that incursion was seeing, on top of the clearing, a *mamacha*—an adult indigenous woman that had not abandoned her traditional dress—seated as if this space was her natural place. The fleas, which would have fled in terror and been looking desperately to feed on the first person they found, didn't seem to bother her. I know that fleas are cunning animals. I have that experience because a few days ago, on the roof of one of the rented houses, I was attacked again by hundreds of them. At that time, a few days ago, I had been raising close to a dozen cats, which gave birth all the time, permitting me, despite my university studies, to stand with some frequency at the door of the supermarkets.

But now there is the possibility of making a filmed autobiography about myself. In front of the camera, once and for all, I am going to leave behind all the masks that I have had to create for myself to continue writing. From the image of the child locked in a mental institution, from which the idea of a series of visits to some public baths so that his mother could take advantage of his naked body, to the performance of marionette numbers to avoid the judgements of eviction. I don't know, however, how a Muslim community in the West can be presented before the camera, the implementation of a series of Sufi rituals in the midst of a society totally foreign to its principles. What is there of truth and what is there of lie in each of the three representations, in each of the three autobiographical moments—*My Skin, Luminous; The Sheikha's True Illness*; and *A Character in Modern Appearance*—that I have presented here? Knowing is entirely irrelevant. There are many characters that are true to life, that is true. A personal history that has to do with the lineage of Italian fascists that I come from, a sick secretary, the impossibility of our making up a normal family. The necessity of erasing any trace of the past, to blur a determined identity as much as possible, based principally on the negation of the time and space that should supposedly correspond to me. Changing tradition, name, history, nationality, religion has been constant in my life. But not to create new institutions to ascribe myself to. Simply to allow the text to manifest in all its possibilities. Most of all, this is made more evident in *The Sheikha's True Illness*, the second period of my autobiography, a story in which a series of dreams experienced over the course of many years are the constitutive element of the fiction. They continue being, that's true, inalterable images. The presence of those bodies' deformation, the missing members with the paraphernalia, so dense and complicated, that that phenomenon typically carries with it. The apparition of an incurable and fatal illness, already anticipated by me myself in texts like *Beauty Salon* and *Blind Poet*. The games with sexual identities. The changing, without any solution of continuity, from being a child exhibited on the outskirts of the tomb of a Muslim saint, into the father of a family, from a fat pig thief, or an indeterminate person, out of touch with their sex and age, who is additionally subjugated by an intransigent father. All to arrive nowhere but at the figure of a timid teenager with square glasses, the only one of all of them that seems real to me, who very soon decides to renounce communion with the others—this occurred in the first years of secondary school—to seek refuge in the company of a group of domestic animals, who would have to give her some answer. This journey seems only to have served to some years later convert me simply into a contemporary writer, who almost without noticing offered up his life, not to the raising of animals nor to a series of spiritual exercises capable of giving his existence a more dreamlike dimension, but that his true desire wound up being the word, not just creating it but sharing it with a group of future writers that, week after week, meet up, with an admirable faith, to try to unravel the hidden meaning of some texts. And to share it also with two or three friends whose choice was similar: that of writing just to write.

That is perhaps why, despite the widely scattered life I've led, I am now happy. Without the baggage of emotions, family, nation, or identity. At my age something has happened in my circumstance that makes me feel like this. I think that it is the best state in which to practice my work. Without worrying any longer that the strangeness of my body might be exhibited even naked, like a popular attraction, without thinking too much about the vestments necessary to plunge into the dances of the dervishes. Without the miniskirts or high heels being a problem, nor the look I must display to fulfill the role of a German girl's boyfriend who desperately seeks an absurd car, or to represent a funny marionette with her ankles and wrists tied with a transparent string. This change of perspective has to have been influenced, in a decisive manner what's more, by the promised filmed biography.

Seeing myself recreated in another format, I will liberate myself, among other things, from the necessity of stealing money from my father's almost empty wallet. May my nephews fend for themselves however they can. It makes me not care whether they stop receiving their candies. They have their father for that, who, I must finally say it, is a builder that has never raised a house. That, to the contrary, agreed with my father about the destruction of the family home, making use of his incipient knowledge as a surveyor. I never knew why he did it—my father, I mean. Perhaps to demonstrate that destiny is discovered on top of everything else. Or perhaps to flaunt his incipient knowledge, learned at a local annex of the veterinary school from which, with my friend from school, I stole a pig that was later served as dinner to a group of clandestine gamblers. I think that my state is one of the best to be had. I notice it because the optimal places where I usually write are hospitals—where they intern me from time to time, airports, planes, trains, and writer's residencies. I never started to think about what would have happened to me upon writing on the chicken farm that belonged to my uncle, my father's cousin—who wound up committing suicide after his business was a true disaster. It would be good, in order to make the filmed biography that's intended, to take a trip to the mountain where that small farm was located. The misty cantinas from downtown, which make up part of the scenery of my first book, must also be recreated. The house situated in the zone known as *The Descent* must also be visited, today converted into a place for the sale of regional food, where the poet César Moro spent his last years. That one must be the primary setting of my second book. Another text, the third one, takes place in a neighborhood called Miramar. The fourth comes from my investigations undertaken in nightclubs frequented by transsexuals. The fifth has as its axis two characteristic neighborhoods, one that has a beach where you can swim, ride waves, and play water sports, and the other one inhabited by an emerging middle class. The sixth book is an attempt to represent, from a certain point of view, the extreme politicization that I lived through at the universities where my studies took place, which is the reason why many of its chapters take place, at least mentally, on its outskirts. These books, despite the concrete settings that the film will certainly show, were originally written from no-land and no-space, and for that same reason, coincide with a number of lived experiences of a personal nature. I begin to experience a true time that truly does not exist, and which for that same reason I consider to be more real than the real, only when I write from my dreams. This is the theme not just of one chapter of this autobiography, the second one, but of some books that are about to appear, and which I intend not to sign as Mario Bellatin, the naked boy with big genitals, the character preoccupied with the destiny of the hairless dogs, the girl-old lady impacted by the demolition of her family home, or the boy with square glasses that dreamed of having a German girlfriend, but simply as Salám. Abdús Salám, rather, the Son of Peace. But I think that all these projects, most of all the editing of that new book of dreams, are literary enterprises that I am not going to be able to bring to fruition. In recent times my mind becomes more and more dispersed. I have forgotten the marionette dances, I hardly remember the rat that I carried on my shoulder at the metro stations anymore, nor that man who sold hamsters and closed me in a bedroom. I don't have any certainty either of having had an appointment that day at the hospital where they admitted the sheikha, nor of having ever been interested in Renault cars. I don't know what happened to my person when my testicles no longer attracted the women at the baths. Neither do I know the reason why many of my friends criticized the decision when I affixed the cage to the bicycle. Neither did I ever stop to think what would have happened had I written about the dark details of the type of chicken farm that belonged to my uncle, an old relative of my father, who wound up dying after his business was a true disaster. I want, from here on, to reproduce the fragmented images that surround me and which don't lead, like my life, anywhere. Although to accomplish it I must use, though for the last time, my funny little fantasy doll outfit.

The Bride Stripped Bare by Her Bachelors, Even:

A Translator's Note

In translating the second section of *The Large Glass*, I was struck by how much the author's reflections on Sufism reminded me of the inexactitude of the process at hand, that of translation. In *The Sheikha's True Illness*, Bellatin writes,

> *Sufism posits that we have completely forgotten the ideal world we come from. The voices that came out of the mosque told us that our labor is in remembering, in remembrance. The heart must remember, remember its entire previous life.*

Like the heart of the mystic embracing the ideal world she has forgotten—and here I posit that having completely forgotten the ideal, original text is essential to the process—the translator must remember the translation's previous life, must rediscover the essence of the original.

In that same section of the book, Bellatin speaks of "writing as prophecy." I'd like to suggest a corollary principle: translation as divination. Between Bellatin's original composition, made entirely of his words, and this translation, made entirely of mine, lies a process that ultimately results in a text that is both entirely its own and entirely a reflection of the ideal text it came from, something, in my own experience, no matter how technically or scientifically approached, cannot be categorized as other than a mystical experience.

The Large Glass is a bride stripped bare, further exposed—exposed to the level of its very syntax and lexicon—through the act of translation. It's my attempt at divination, at divining an entirely new, entirely same English-language book from the Spanish-language original. Any errors, omissions, or additions are the result of that inexact process, and I accept responsibility for them as necessary functions of my divination.

ABOUT THE AUTHOR

MARIO BELLATIN is a Mexican Sufi who studied theology in Peru and film in Cuba. His dozens of novellas have won all of Mexico's major writing prizes. His novel *The Uruguayan Book of the Dead*, forthcoming from Phoneme Media, won the 2015 José María Arguedas Prize, Cuba's most important prize for fiction. He was a guest curator of Documenta 13.

ABOUT THE TRANSLATOR

DAVID SHOOK's collection *Our Obsidian Tongues* was longlisted for the International Dylan Thomas Prize in 2013. His many published translations include books by Mexican writers Tedi López Mills, Víctor Terán, Salvador Novo, and Kyn Taniya.